ONE -SHOT PUBLICATION

MUST KEEP A GUN 3

3rd of 8 Books

3 In the Dopest Series Ever

A Novel By:

Robert D. Williams

DISCLAIMER

This book is a work of fiction. Any reference to real people, events, establishments or locals are intended to give the fiction a sense of reality and authenticity. Any names, characters, and incidents occurring in the work are either the product of the author's imagination, or are used fictitiously, and those that include fictionalized events, and incidents that involve real people, and any character that happens to share the name of a person who is an acquaintance of the author, past or present, is purely coincidental and in no way intended to be an actual account involving that person. This book is a complete work of fiction, created from the author's imagination and for entertainment purposes only.

ONE SHOT PUBLICATIONS
2233 5TH STREET
MUSKEGON HEIGHTS, MICHIGAN 49444

Email: ONESHOTPUBLICATIONS@GMAIL.COM

Website: WWW.ONESHOTPUBLICATIONSLLC.COM

Prologue

At ADX supermax prison in Colorado, 4 prison guards walked down one of the prison's dark hallways. It was just past midnight, lights were out, and all 4 guards held their keys so they wouldn't jingle and disturb the sleeping prisoners. When they made it to the door of cell they had come for they stopped and looked at the door. They had been sent to retrieve a very important prisoner for secret transport. The lead guard looked down at his clipboard, he flashed his light on it, up at the door then he looked over his shoulder at the other three men in his crew.

"We go in, cuff him, and once we make sure the restraints are secure we back him out nice and slow then get him off to the airlift A.S.A.P."

Their mission was to get Money out of the prison and to transport without causing a riot. Their tactical strategy was stealth. The lead guard keyed the cell door open and flooded the room with his flashlight. Money was siting at his desk. His back was wide, fully tattooed, and facing them. The ink on big BPN tattoo on his back glistened in the light. He looked over his shoulder at the guards. His face was stone.

The guards looked at one another, then back to him.

Money smiled and turned back to the wall. "Turn that light off in my cell," he said.

The guard turned the light to the ground. "Yeah sure. Got some good news for you."

"And what's that?" Money asked with his back still to them.

The guard held up a pair of handcuffs, belly chains and shackles. "You've been granted a transfer out of this shit hole. And we've come to transport you."

Money turned in the chair. In the dim light the guards saw all the wounds and tattoos on his chest and stomach. "I wasn't told about a transfer."

"I got orders on this clipboard that tells me you'r supposed to be on con-air tonight and transported to your next facility."

"And what about my CO defendant?" Money asked. He had stepped farther back into the shadows deeper in the back of the cell.

The guard shrugged, looked over his shoulder at his co-workers, then back down at the clipboard. "This is the transfer list right here that the air marshals sent, and it doesn't say anything about your co-defendant. Just you."

One of the other guards stepped up and pulled a taser from his waist and aimed it at Money's chest. The red beam was on his solar plexus. "Either you cuff up on your own, or I tase you, and then we cuff you our way. Either way it goes you're getting cuffed and on that plane."

Money stood up and all four guards took a step back, even the one with the taser gun and threats. They all had heard the stories and knew what Money was capable of. He had been calm for the last few years, but the prison staff and every inmate nation wide knew about Money's other side all too well. He laughed and the guards relaxed then Money slid a shirt over his head then approached the guards with his arms together and extended out to the lead officer and said, "Go ahead Tillman, cuff me."

Tillman swallowed hard and removed the cuffs from his belt. He slowly latched them around Money's wrist and clinked them shut, then got down on one knee and secured the shackles on his ankles. Then all four guards backpedaled out of the room and back out into the hallway. The guard with the taser still had his aim up and the red dot was in Money's chest as he walked out. One by one cell lights came on and eyes peered out of cell doors. Even through the steel of the cell doors the eyes still sent chills down the officer's spines.

When they were out of the hallway they passed through a door and was in a dress out room where they had Money strip, walk through a metal detector naked, then put on a solid white jumpsuit made out of some type of stiff paper fabric.

One last stop at a desk, the guards signed papers and then turned Money over to the care of the United States air marshals. The marshals escorted Money through a door at the back of the prison then through another door and they were outside. He stopped momentarily and stared up at the sky, it had been a long time since he had seen the outside world. In ADX he was never allowed out of his cell, especially never allowed outside. It had bee 10 years since he'd had a breath of fresh air not fed to him artificially through a vent. Occasionally he did get an hour out in the recreation cage, which was just a 10 foot square maze of cement walls and steel grating for a roof.

One of the air marshals pushed him in the back. He stumbled forward and mugged the marshal over his shoulder then turned back and stared at the bus, at the tinted windows and listened to the low hum of its motor. The hydraulic door pulled back and as best as he could Money climbed the three steps with the shackles on his ankles. Once on the bus he looked down the aisle at the only two faces. He didn't recognize either one of the prisoners. He found an empty seat and was on his way. The walk down the aisle was difficult because of the shackles but he just took his time and moved each leg forward inch by inch. He took a seat in the middle of the bus and the guards took their positions behind the wheel and at the very back of the bus in a specially built cage.

The bus lurched forward, made a wide turn into traffic and was on its way. Money eyed the prisoner toward the front of the bus. When they locked stares the white boy nodded and Money nodded back, then Money turned and looked at the prisoner in the back of the bus. He was a young light skinned cat with a short cut. Money nodded but the youngster didn't nod back. Instead his eyes narrowed and he looked closer at Money. Money turned back in his seat and faced the front of the bus.

Money took in the scenery and enjoyed the ride through the country in the middle of the night. It had been years. They took the highway and headed for the airport. It felt weird riding in a car, seeing trees, or normal people and smelled the gas from the gas stations.

His mind turned to his co - defendant, Paper, who was also in ADX, but they hadn't seen one another in years even though they were in the same building. They had only spoken to one another once and that was because they had ended up in recreation cages next to one another. The conversation had been through a vent in the SHU cage.

They had made a pat that if they ever made it in the same room together ever again, that they would escape. Now as his bus traversed the dark road Money wondered where Paper was, if he would ever see him again, and would they ever get their chance. The van pulled up to the back gate of the airport. Once it was let in it made its way to the lit up runway followed by heavy security.

A plane took off in the distance, it's lights and the smoke trail behind it was visible for miles in the night sky even after the plane itself had disappeared.

The bus inched forward at a snail's pace. Money could see the huge plane in front of them on the runway. He knew it was the federal transport plane, or Con - air, because of the duct tape on the wing, and how dull and plane the paint job was. There were no markings or symbols on it, no company logo, it was just an airplane. Black and blue vans were parked off to the side and masked marshals were lined up along the runway with assault rifles and shotguns. They looked menacing in their masks, cargo pants, boots, and bulletproof vests with us marshals written on them.

The van Money was in parked next to the others and at the same time all of the marshals vans unloaded the shackled prisoners from all of the vans, lined them up in a single file line, including Money. Then just like cattle on a farm Money and the others were herded into one of the lines that had already been formed. He took a deep breath and looked at the airplane. At how raggedy it was, at the tape on the wings, the peeling paint, and the wires that he could see were loose. After they all had their mouths, hands and entire body searched they were ushered up the airplane's steps. The shackles bit at their ankles.

On the plane Money looked at the filled rows. Men and women were on their way to either be prosecuted or to finish their time at one of the various federal prisons peppered throughout the country. After the marshals seated them Money just sat back, looked out the window and waited for the plane to take off.

After sitting on the runway for a half an hour the plane finally lurched forward, plane picked up speed quickly, and then was in the air. It punched through the clouds at 30,000 feet.

"You Money ain't you?"

Startled at the voice Money looked to his right. He hadn't paid attention before, but the nigga next to him was the same young light skinned cat that had been on the transport bus with him.

"Who is you, and why you want to know?" Money shot back.

"I'm Ced," the young nigga said and extended his shackled hands as far as he could out to Money for him to shake.

Money was hesitant but shook the man's hand. He froze when he saw the 3 letter tattoo in the crease of the youngster's hand. **BPN**. He jerked his head up and looked into Ced's eyes.

"I'm from Muskegon." Ced said. "Wood Street, and I'm a Black Pirate Nigga."

Money was speechless. He had been in ADX and cut off from the outside world, and most importantly from what he loved and had created. **BPN**. He had heard through the grapevine about it's growth but thought it was just rumors about how much the gang he had created had grown, and spread. Now on a federal airbus he had seen cold hard proof. The last thing he had heard about BPN was the death of Blaze when he'd gotten into the shootout in the club in Muskegon at the hands of the gang out of Flint, the Woodhall Island Boys.

Money raised his shackled hands and with one he touched the BPN tattoo just under his left eye. He looked his young soldier in the eyes. Even after isolation it was easy to step back into his role as leader. "Yeah," he said, "I'm money. Who put you down?"

"Dude named Murda."

The name didn't ring a bell to Money. He looked out of the window at the clouds in the sky. "What can you tell me them about them Flint niggas, the Woodhall Island Boys?"

Ced told him everything he knew firsthand and everything he had heard. How the gang had crept into the streets of Muskegon, and how they now had complete control over a section of the Southside and were recruiting members heavily. "They even flipped some of the BPN homies."

"What about Blaze? They're the ones responsible for Blaze's murder?"

Ced hung his head, lifted back up and shook it. "Yeah, I was there that night in the club, but there wasn't shit anybody could do. Once the shots started the people went crazy and all hell broke loose. The ones that didn't get shot got ran over by the other people. Shit was fucked up."

"Did he have an open casket funeral?" Money asked.

"Yeah, we sent the homie off good."

Money turned to the window with his thoughts on Blaze, his old friend. He turned back to Ced and said, "It was good meeting you lil homie. When you get out make sure them Woodhall niggas pay." It hurt to say the words out loud. He wanted revenge personally but knew he had a life sentence. He knew he wouldn't have the chance to exact revenge and get the actual wet blood on his hands. Blaze was more than a friend, he was his BPN brother too. He fought back tears. Batted them back with the lids of his eyes.

"Is it true that you killed 5 cops and got caught with a 100 keys of dog food?" Ced asked.

Money chuckled under his breath because just like every other urban legend he had heard about him this one had been over exaggerated as well. Someone, or many people somewhere down the line had taken his life and had turned it into a camp fire tale. Probably what they told the little homies at the meetings they had or at initiations. To all BPN members Money and Paper were legends locked off doing life in ADX, but with many legends and prophecies surrounding their names and reputation.

"That's the story you heard huh?"

Ced nodded.

"Well that's false information lil homie." Money told him then held his hands up and showed the chains on his wrists. "But since we stuck on this airplane I guess it's my duty as your big homie, your chief, and leader to tell you the truth, show you the history. So listen close. This is the true story. The story of our beginnings."

Chapter 1

Standing 5 feet 11 inches Money wasn't tall at all but was on the stocky side. His hands were characteristically big because he did push ups on the concrete in front of the trap spot everyday, and sometimes on his knuckles so they were calloused. This was a daily thing since he basically had nothing else to do with his young life but stand on the corner or in front abandoned houses and wait for drug addicts to come through and spend their money. It was always him and Blaze, and they were closer than peas in a pod. As soon as he would come up from his set of push ups he would dust his knuckles off, pull a brush from his pocket, and brushed his waves. The trap house they were in front of was the spot they posted in front of daily. This was their daily routine. Young black hustlers in the hood trying not to get lost in a cold young world.

Neither one had been to school in 2 years and they were only 15, which meant they had dropped out at 13. They played the block tough though. It was their university.

Blaze stood on the porch of a dope fiend's crib and watched a pack of young girls walk down the street. Right in the middle. Blaze laughed and looked at Money. "I get it now."

Money broke his stare from the young girls and looked at Blaze. "What the fuck you get now?"

"Why you pump up your chest everyday at 3:30. That's for shorty in the red huh?" He shook his head and laughed. "After all this time I just now figured that shit out. You a sucker bro."

Money threw the brush at him. "Fuck you nigga. You need to get some pussy. All you think about is selling crack. Grow up nigga. You 15 now it's other shit in the world.

You need to get out more." He walked over and picked up his brush. "And don't watch me, watch t.v."

Blaze was smooth for his age and was a little taller than Money with a bald fade and was dark skinned. The fade always had a slanted part and he kept a smile on his face. Before he dropped out of school and went to the streets he was a star football player and was number 2 in the state chess standings. He was smart and quiet for the most part, and if he didn't know you then you probably would never hear him speak a single word.

Money and Blaze had been brought up together and had been friends since they were in diapers, and back in the day their mothers used to be best friends. Drug addictions have divided them though over the years. Money's momma was a crack addict, cross addicted actually, addicted to both heroin and cocaine. In the last year she had even taken the big step of injecting the heroin with a needle. She was an alcoholic too.

Blaze's momma was addicted too at one point but had beat her addiction. This is when her and Money's mother's relationship grew apart.

"I've been doing a lot of thinking Blaze," Money said.

"About what? I hope you thinking about an aids test since you tricked with that dope fiend last night."

Money stared at Blaze. "All bullshit aside," he said, "I ain't trick with that fiend neither. You tripping. I don't do what you do."

"Why you go in the room with her then?"

"To catch the play stupid."

"Why ya'll was in there so long? You made love to her didn't you?"

Money threw Blaze his middle finger. "Fuck you. Bro, you need to take life a little more serious. This shit real out here." They were both silent for a moment then Money said, "I ain't fuck her aight, but I did get my dick sucked. But you wasting my time with this bullshit, I don't want to talk about that shit. I want to talk about some other shit."

Blaze looked at him with a blank face. "What other shit?"

Money pointed around the neighborhood. "This fucked up life we living. Even at a young age I know this shit ain't right bro."

"So what you saying?"

"We 15 now and we some money getting little niggas but we still out here selling rocks. Look at how everybody divided, how don't nobody live by codes or rules and laws. These niggas out here just living. The whole city is just one big pussy waiting to get fucked. Ain't no way in hell we supposed to be sitting in front of this house everyday interacting with fiends hand to hand and still only where we at."

They were silent for a moment. Blaze broke the silence and said, "Yeah, you right this is some bullshit."

"So I came up with a plan."

"And what kind of plan is this you done came up with?"

"We go to the stash, grab all the bread we got and go and see Big World. He'll match us whatever we spend if we spend enough money. As long as we stay at the little kid level we gone be on the little kid level and get treated just like it."

Blaze thought for a moment. Turned his back to Money and stared at the rundown houses on the block. He turned back to Money and shrugged. "Let's do it."

The phone call to Big World was quick. Money closed the phone and since the neighborhood was filled with abandoned houses they had learned to utilize them for all their needs while in the hood. They used them to bag up, smoke, get pussy, throw underground parties, and the ones they never told anyone about they used for stash spots.

They slipped through the backdoor and put the board back. In the basement they went back to the farthest room, pulled a brick from the wall and Money pulled out a metal can. He pulled a money roll from the can and held it in front of both their faces. "Today we go from hustling rocks to pushing weight and getting real money."

Blaze nodded with a smile. The money in the can was all the money they had saved on the block selling crack. Money stuffed the cash in his pocket and put the empty can back in its spot then they hurried up the steps out the door. They hurried back through the abandoned yard, the field, and back to the trap house they always stood in front of and had claimed as their own.

A few minutes later Big World pulled up. His music shook everything on the block. Made it rattle and vibrate. Every time he pulled up to any scene all eyes were on him and his truck. He was the man and he knew it and didn't try to hide it. He jumped out and stepped in front of his truck and smiled with his colorful teeth shiny like crazy in the sun. "Which one of you niggas riding with me to the spot. I'll bring you right back."

Money turned to Blaze. "I'mma slide with him. I'll be right back." He started for Big World's truck turned back to Blaze and said, "And put the dope up. Don't be standing on the corner with that shit on you." He climbed in the truck.

A dude named Lester was in the passenger seat. Money could only see the top of his head and the bottom of the liquor bottle when he turned it up and took deep swallows.

Blaze and Money eyed one another through the window as the truck pulled from the curb.

"Me and Blaze been getting money with you for a minute now," Money said and watched both men's eyes focus on him in the truck's mirrors. "But we been running through the little shit we've been buying too quick. We think it's time that we graduated." He dug in his pocket and extended him and Blaze's savings to the front seat.

Big World looked at it. "That's your whole stash huh?" He nudged Lester on the passenger side with his elbow. "These little niggas ready to jump up to the big leagues. I knew this day was coming. I feel like a proud daddy watching his kids graduate."

The truck turned onto a dirt road filled with rocks that crunched under the truck's tires. The sound of the rocks crunching alerted 2 pit bulls that ran to the front gate of Big World's house. They barked, snarled and barked their teeth angrily.

World parked the truck and all climbed out. Big World and Lester entered the fence but Money stopped just outside of it and stared at the dogs. Big World grabbed one of them and Lester the other by the collar. He laughed. "They ain't gone bite you little nigga... well not as long as you with us or I don't give them the word to shred your ass." He said and with his free hand he offered the bottle of liquor to Money over the fence.

Money shook his head no. Lester snatched the bottle and turned it up then waddled with the dog in his grips to the backyard. "Follow us," he told Money over his shoulder.

Money followed them to the back of the house and waited as they put the dogs up then followed Lester and Big World inside the house. Inside Big World flipped on a light and Lester stumbled off deeper into the house.

"This way," World told Money. He led the way into the kitchen.

Money stopped at the threshold of the kitchen and looked around. He tossed the money on the table. The house was basically empty, only a refrigerator and a big ass pyrex jar turned upside down drying on the countertop.

In the distance Lester could be heard vomiting, and he was struggling. Mostly dry heaves.

"I told that nigga to slow the fuck down on all that liquor," Big world snapped and shook his head. "Niggas don't be listening. One day they'll start." He went in the refrigerator and came out with a bag, sat it on the table and looked at Money. "How much bread you say that was?"

"I never said, but it's 55 hundred."

Big World laughed at the snappy line. "Little funny nigga huh? Okay, do any one of you niggas know how to cook up cocaine into crack?" He studied Money's face. "I ain't think so. Ya'll wouldn't have been on that block selling rocks that long. You niggas would have been got the concept of the dope game, and we would've been had this conversation."

"We both willing to learn though. Pay a nigga if we have to even."

"Pay a nigga to teach you right, not to cook for you, right?" He opened the Walmart bag and pulled out a kilo of cocaine and held it up. "This a brick right here. You ever seen one before?"

Money shook his head no.

"This shit right here will make a dead man move and I'll give it to you just how I get it. Straight off the brick." He sat the brick back inside the Walmart bag and went back inside the vegetable bin inside the refrigerator.

The sound of Lester throwing up intensified in the distance.

Money pulled a pistol from his hoody pocket and even though his hands were wet and shaking he took aim at Big World and steadied his hands just enough so that when he pulled the trigger he hit his target. Again and again. Act bullet burrowed into Big World with a smacking sound. Big World dropped to the ground in a pool of his own blood.

Money stepped up and kicked Big World over then looked down at him and in his eyes. He took aim again, this time at Big world's forehead and pulled the trigger then turned and hurried down the hall. The hallway was short and skinny, and the bathroom door was wide open. Lester was on his knees and hugging the toilet. He turned his head and stared at Money. His eyes dropped down to the smoking gun in Money's hand

He panicked and tried to get up but vomit d at the same time and in the chunky sticky liquid. On his way or the floor he hit his head on the toilet. He was face down on the floor dead and motionless. Money stepped over him, took aim, and with his hand steadier than before he put a bullet in the back of Lester's head. He opened his eyes and looked down at Lester's body. He dry heaved and stumbled backwards out of the bathroom, into the kitchen where he grabbed the plastic bags from off the table, emptied out the rest of the dope in the vegetable bin inside then looked at Big World's body. He squatted over the dead man, then turned the gun around so that he was holding the barrel. He opened World's mouth and looked at the colorful rainbow teeth then cocked back and hit him as hard as he could with the butt of his pistol. With trembling hands he picked up the bloody teeth, tossed them in a bag and hurried out of the back door.

Outside the dogs jumped at him. He stopped in his tracks but the dogs were caught by their chains. Money hurried to the alley, and once in the alley he broke into an all-out run.

A few blocks over Money exited the alley and entered his brother's backyard, hurried to the door and let himself inside. His breathing was hard and his arms were filled with Walmart bags of cocaine but he let himself collapse and fall back onto the door. He was shaking badly and his mind was racing. He gathered himself and went to the basement, hid the bags and went back upstairs. When he walked in the living room where his brother and his company was his brother took one look at him and got to his feet and turned the music off. The women that had been dancing turned and looked at him.

"What the fuck?" One of them said.

"Bitch is this your house?" Tae waited for her to answer but she said nothing. "Thoughts so. Everybody gotta go. I got some shit I need to do."

No one else argued just grabbed their belongings and exited through the back door. Money was alone in the living room when his brother walked back in.

"Money what's up, what the fuck wrong with you? Why you got that look on your face?"

Money turned and faced his brother. His brother saw the blood on his shirt and his trembling hands.

Money hesitated then said, "I killed Big World and Lester."

"What you mean you killed Big World?"

Money shook his head and stared blankly at his brother. "I killed him, they dead."

Tae fell back on the couch and clutched his face in his hands. "This ain't for you Money. I never wanted this for you."

"Well I got it. Ain't no turning back." He squeezed the tears away that wanted to fall from his eyes. He didn't want to feel. "The past is the past. Ain't that what momma used to always say?"

Tae moved his hands from his face and looked up at his younger brother.

"Follow me," Money told his brother. He led him to the basement, to the money, gun, and jewelry. Tae looked at it all. "When he showed it to me the gun just came out. I don't know what the fuck happened."

chapter 2

Blaze stood on the corner, him and his girlfriend Alicia. They were under the street light and he was behind her with his pressed against her ass and his arms wrapped around her waist. His lips were on her neck and her homegirls were staring at them with jealousy and envy in their eyes.

"I called you earlier but you didn't answer my call," Alicia said and looked at Blaze over her shoulder. "What was you doing that you couldn't answer your phone?"

Blaze shrugged. "I don't know," he said. "I ain't see your call though."

An unmarked car turned the corner and crept their way. Blaze let his arms fall from around Alicia. At that moment he remembered the dope, their stash, was in his pocket. He turned and started down the street towards the house they trapped at.

Alicia stood there..

The unmarked car pulled up alongside Blaze. Right up on the curb. 2 detectives. The detective on the passenger side jumped out before the car's tires stopped rolling. Blaze sped up and tucked his head. The other detective slapped the car in gear and jumped out.

"Hands on the hood," he said and snatched Blaze up, swung him in a quick circle and threw him on the hood of the unmarked car. "I don't know where the fuck you think you're walking off to so fast! You know it ain't that easy."

Blaze stared at the narcotics officer dressed in plain clothes. This wasn't their first run in, but the exact opposite, it was a daily thing.

They had been watching from down the street for hours just waiting for him to leave the safety of the traphouse they used. It was impossible for Blaze to run. The detective slapped a pair of cuffs around Blaze's wrist. Then the detective spun him around and went in his pockets. He stared in his eyes as he searched. Every pocket was empty.

"Told you I don't roll like that!" Blaze shouted.

The detective came out of Blaze's front right pocket slowly and squeezed between his fingers was a bag of crack. He dangled it in front of Blaze's face.

"Been waiting to catch you down bad for a long time. This what happens when Money ain't around to do all the thinking huh? You fucked up this time." The detective read Blaze his rights. "You're under arrest for possession with intent to deliver crack cocaine." There was a smile on his face that spread wider with every word he spoke.

Everyone out on the block watched the cops throw Blaze in the back of unmarked car.

"It won't be long before we catch Money up in some shit too and he'll be right next to you wherever you end up." He closed the door and stared at the crowd. His dick got hard.

\#

Tae turned the car him and Money were in onto the block only to see the unmarked turn off the street followed by a marked car. Money jumped out and hurried over everyone that had been watching the police activity. Money turned his stare from the end of the block to Alicia. He closed out the distance between him and her.

"Alicia where Blaze at?"

With trembling lips and her arms folded across her body she looked blanky at the corner, down at the end of the block Money himself had just been staring at. Money followed her stare. Without another word he turned and climbed back in the car with his brother.

Tae looked at his Money from behind the steering wheel. "What's up with Blaze?" He asked.

"They got him," was all Money could get out without tears falling from his eyes.

Tae pulled the car from the scene. "Do you know what happen?"

Money shrugged. "I don't know. Only thing I do know to do now is get money."

"That ain't what I mean bro and you know it. The heat about to come down. Detectives gone be all over everything and if they know you left with Big World and that nigga Lester then they gon' be on you. We gotta get rid of anything and everything that can tie you to what happened tonight."

Money sat up straight in the passenger seat. "Look, you my big brother and all, but I knew what I was doing. Shit wasn't no accident. But you right, I do need to get shit together just in case."

\#

Tae drove them to a low key spot under a bridge and where there was a flowing river.

They both got out. Tae took the gun, wiped it off, then tossed the it inside the quick moving water. It wasn't clear but not murky either. They watched it sink then get caught by the current, get carried off and disappear down stream.

Tae turned to his little brother. "No matter how long it takes or how inconvenient always handle business first, be secure, and take the extra steps. If not it'll cost you a bunch of years in the pen. And for future references little bro always use revolvers."

"Why?" Money asked.

"Because of the shell casings. With a revolver nothing is left at the scene. Nothing to trace back and connect to other shit or to you. a dead man tells no tales... unless you leave evidence then dead niggas get to talking a lot. And it get worse when you don't destroy all the other shit that can tie you in with it."

They climbed back in the car and went to Tae's house.

Chapter 3

Money woke up early, that's if he had slept at all. Both Big World and Lester were on his mind, and it kept stirring him from his sleep. He was at his girlfriend Tricia's house, but when he looked around she wasn't in the bed with him. He got up and went to the living room. Tricia and Alicia were at the dining room table. Alicia was crying, her eyes were red when she looked up at Money.

Money's phone rang when he answered it was Man Man and he was outside. Money told him to come in and hung up the phone. Man Man didn't take long to walk through the door, and when he did his face was twisted with anger.

"Got some news," he said.

"And what news is that?" Money asked.

"They found a gun on Blaze plus the dope."

Money thought quick and hard. "We from the same hood ain't we Man Man?"

Man Man's eyes turned to slits as he squinted at the question. "Of course. Why you ask that?"

At 20 years old Man Man was 5 years older than Money and damn near an O.G. in the hood. Just surviving alone gave him that title. He had put in a lot work though along the way. He didn't know where Money was going with the conversation but he knew that Money was trying to read him. Study him. Clock him.

"I got some shit I'm putting together," Money said. "I'm thinking I want you to be a part of it."

"What type of shit you talking about?"

Money smiled, inhaled deeply, then exhaled. "Just know it's big, real big, and when it happen, this shit will make the most noise this city has ever seen."

"And when you make that noise," Man Man said, "I'll be there at your side making sure mothafuckas hear it loud and clear!"

Both Alicia and Tricia stared at Man Man. Both were awed at his devotion. Money nodded to Man Man and Man Man exited using the same door he had came in.

For a young nigga Money was ahead of time and he himself knew it. He turned and hurried in the room before the girls saw the tears fall from his eyes and slide down his face. He thought about Blaze and wished he could set back the hands of time. He wished that Blaze could see what he had done for them, and what the future held for them.

Even though Blaze was locked up Money was going to make sure that he still reaped the benefits of their relationship. Their brotherhood.From everything that they had built. Money would still keep their mission, goals, get their money up, and help him take care of his girl if she stood by his side.

In all of his 15 years of life he had never seen 1 person escape the hood, only people try and fool themselves, but not put the work in or make the right moves. He told himself right then and there that he would be one of the few that did escape and make it out by any means necessary. Slide through the cracks.

Chapter 4

The murders had made Money cold. Even though he had never really had a childhood he knew any chance of ever having a normal life had been lost to him and had died with Big World and Lester. Dead and buried.

Blaze was locked up and juveniles weren't allowed to get bonds according to the law, plus he had other problems that he had to deal with. They had charged him as an adult which meant they really wanted him gone and off the streets. They didn't give a fuck how young he was, nor did they give a fuck about any of the young boys they locked up. Blaze attended his first court date as scheduled and everyone was there and watched from the pews.

Money, Alicia, and Tricia sat in the wooden pews and hung onto every word the prosecutor and Blaze's lawyer shouted and argued back and forth.

Money looked at the detectives. It was hard to duck them since they made it their purpose to sit 2 seats in back of him. When he turned and looked at them they both smiled and waved.

One of them leaned forward and said loud enough so Money could hear, "Better stay out of the way or I guarantee you'll be in a cell next to him. Just listen. We know you were the last person to be in the truck with Big World and Lester. The streets talk."

Money ignored them and kept his focus straight ahead on the court proceeding.

"You can ignore us all you want, but when we get what we need we'll be to see you." He slid a newspaper with Big World and Lester's murder on the front page over his shoulder. "Something for you to think about while you wait for us to come and snatch you up." He retook his seat.

Money got to his feet, and with Tricia at his side he left the court room.

Alicia stayed to finish Blaze's court proceeding.

The detective followed Money and Tricia out of the courtroom and into the hallway. Money stopped and faced them.

"Would ya'll stop following me please?" He asked and pulled out his cell phone, pressed record and laughed at the cops. With the phone recording he used his free hand and teeth and shredded the newspaper then let it fall to the floor. "Fuck your article, and fuck ya'll. Like I said, stop following me." Again he turned and walked off with Tricia at his side.

#

When he made it to Tricia's crib he got a pen and a piece of paper, sat down, and started a letter to his friend.

Chapter 5

despite Blaze being a juvenile he had adult charges and in the system he was grown. They placed him in isolation and joe his, in isolation. He was housed in the juvenile part of the jail and not at the youth home. All across the board he had gotten fucked over and he knew it.

Where he was housed was filled with young wild niggas, the ones that had been on the streets doing all the killing and robbing. He was with the worst of the worst and not the calm. The only cat he knew was a dude from his hood named Big Vicious. They had grown up together but had grown apart over the years. Last he had heard about Big Vicious is that he had went crazy and had started a click called APE MOB.

Then there was Quan, Quan had already gotten sentenced and was on his way to one of the juvenile joints on the east coast for a couple of years.

Blaze was shirtless and lying on his bunk when Q.B. started talking shit. "Fuck you all stressed out for?"

Blaze sat up in his bunk and looked at Q.B. and Vicious. "Did they pass out mail yet? Fuck what ya'll talking about."

"They ain't pass it out today they made a list instead. Your name on it."

Without another word Blaze rushed from the cell and to the officer's station. "You got some mail for Banks?" He asked.

The guard dropped his feet off the desk and flipped through the stack of mail until he found the mail and gave it to Blaze. Smiling from ear to ear Blaze hurried to his cell and ripped the letter open. The first thing he pulled out was a newspaper clipping. It was of the double murder of Big World and Lester. He read the article slow and under his breath, then pulled Money's letter out of the envelope and read it too under his breath. He wondered why would Money send him the clipping, but then he studied the clipping. He looked at the time of death in the article. Then remembered what Big World's real name was and Lester was just Lester. It was the same time on his police report, and everything else matched up. He had watched some coverage of the murders but had never paid it any attention or thought twice about Money being involved. Blaze let the letter fall to his lap and wondered what had happened, and then he wondered what had prompted Money to do it if he did it. But then he already knew what it was. It was the conversation they had just had in front of their spot.

He reopened Money's letter.

:To my nigga Blaze,

What's good my nigga? I wish you was out here. Shit about to change for the better. We ain't poor no more, and it all happened overnight. I really can't explain but you can do the math and read between the lines without spelling lessons I hope. If I shine you shine. We all shine. We shine together.

Me and Tricia been keeping Alicia close to us. I don't know if she told you but she got a surprise for you.

Me and Tricia all the way together now. I ain't been staying at your spot no more but at Tricia's house and laying low. Staying out the way.

Write me back nigga. I love you fool.

Love, Money your brother:

Money was no killer, but Blaze had saw something in his eyes when they'd had that conversation. He opened the letter from Alicia and the first sentence made him drop it because the tears that fell from his eyes fell fast and hard.

Alicia was pregnant.

Blaze cried like a baby and he didn't give a fuck who saw him or was watching.

Chapter 6

A chick named Kendra was the senior hood rat around Money's hood. She was older and her spot was always open to the homies form the hood whether they needed a room to sleep in, fuck, a spot to cut up dope, cook up dope, basically whatever the dope boys needed she provided. Even a shot of pussy if that's what was needed. Niggas even sold dope out of her shit, just had the fiends meet them in the back. She was 18 years old, still young, but older than Money and the homies he kept around.

Money knocked on the door. Kendra opened it in a wife beater only long enough to cover her upper body. Her ass was fully exposed and her house shoes were furry with her toes out. The paint on them were pink like the fur on the house shoes.

"What's up Money?" She asked. "Everybody's here waiting for you. Come on in." She stepped to the side.

Money stepped in, hugged her, then went into the living room. She closed the door behind him with a smile on her face. Everyone knew she had a thing for him.

It was late and Boo Boo was asleep on the couch with a chick named Precious wrapped in his arms. Her ass cheeks were hanging from the bottom of her shorts.

Youngin was asleep on the other couch, and Cuz was asleep in the armchair tucked in the corner. Money kicked the couch, then the chair and the loveseat. Everybody woke up rubbing their eyes.

Man Man walked in and stood behind Money.

The females got up and walked out of the room.

When they were gone Money looked at everyone of the guys individually. "You niggas woke? Because if not we can wait to do this another day. I don't want to feel like I'm the only one dedicated in this room."

Everyone present looked at one another to see if anyone opposed. No one said a word. They all returned their attention to Money.

"Alright since I got no objections," Money said then reached in the bag and pulled out one of the kilos from Big World and sat it on the coffee table in front of everyone, and for all to see. It shined like diamonds.

They all sat up and gawked at the dope on the table.

"I want to take shit over," Money said. "I want to take over the whole dope game in the city."

They all looked at him sideways. None of them understood. But one thing was certain, his words and the show of the dope had everyone's full attention.

Man Man stepped forward with his arms folded across his chest. "All you gotta do is give me the word. Tell me what to do. Where to go." He shrugged. "Who to hit. I'm with you."

Money nodded to Man Man and let him know that he had taken in what he had said.

Man Man's eyes fell down to the kilo. He had never saw more than a few ounces before and it showed on his face. He was a loyal nigga and had influence in his hood and throughout the city plus he had a good mouthpiece. The reputation he had for violence was well known too. Next to Blaze, Money felt deep down inside that Man Man was the person to keep next to him.

"In 3 days there will be a meeting and more of the plan will be laid out." Money told his crowd. "If you want in show up to the meeting and then and there everybody will know exactly what's up."

Kendra stepped in the room and signaled to Money that she needed to have a word with him. Money took his eyes from her and put them back on his guys. "I'll be right back."

He stepped in the small hallway where Kendra was waiting for him. "What's up?"

She grabbed his hand and pulled him into her bedroom. She closed and locked the door then turned to him. "I want you."

She lifted the wife beater over her head and let it fall to the floor.

Money stared at the wife beater on the floor then up at her. "You stopped me from talking real shit to show me some titties?" He turned and walked out of the bedroom. He didn't even close the door behind him, just left her there naked and staring.

Chapter 7

The next day Money awoke to his cell phone ringing. He looked at the number but didn't recognize it answered anyway. It was the detectives, both of them on speaker and talking at the same time. He looked over at the other side of the bed at Kendra, she was still asleep. She was half covered by her comforter. Her eyes opened softly.

"Why are you calling my phone? And how did you get my number?" Money asked.

The detectives laughed. Neither said a word.

Money hung up.

They called back.

Money answered even though he knew he shouldn't have.

"We need you to come down for questioning."

Money hesitated but then said, " Yeah whatever I'll see y'all within the hour," and hung up. He picked the phone right back up and made a call then slipped into his clothes. When he was dressed he looked at Kendra who was watching him. "No breakfast?" He asked her. "Don't worry about it, I'll stop at McDonalds on my way down to the police station."

She flung the cover off of her. "So this was just a one time thing?" She asked him without looking at him. She looked straight ahead with an attitude.

"Kendra you know I got a bitch don't you?"

"Yeah but-"

"Ain't no buts."

"But I ain't tripping on that, you ain't even let me finish. I'm with playing the sideline, but I just don't want you playing me all the way."

He eased over the bed and with the tips of his fingers he caressed her chin. "Look, if you can play the sideline, which is your position anyway, then we good."

She smiled and leaned in for a kiss but a horn blew outside. Money got up to see who it was. She fell on the floor on the side of the bed. It was Money's ride. He turned back to her but had to look down to the floor. She blushed.

He contained his laugh and said, "I'll come back over here later okay?" He didn't wait for her response. He walked out of the room. On his way out the front door he dropped a Walmart bag in Man Man's lap.

"I'll be back," he told Man Man. "Police called and said they want to holla at me. I'm about to go down there and see what they got to say."

Outside he climbed in the car with his brother Tae and they pulled from the curb. They rode in silence but when the station was a block away and in sight Tae lowered the volume on the music.

"When they call you down to the station for questioning instead of hunting you down like an animal that usually mean they don't got shit on you and need you to tell on yourself." He looked to the passenger seat at his brother. That mean don't say shit when you go in there but you want to see your lawyer."

Tae parked in the station's parking lot and they watched as a snitch named C.D. walked out of the front doors. They could tell he was nervous. His head was tucked and he avoided eye contact with their car.

They followed him with their stares until he climbed in his car and pulled from the parking lot.

Money opened the door and got out.

"I ain't going in. I'm staying out here." Tae said before Money closed the door. "Remember what I told you. If they need you to talk that mean that they ain't got shit."

Money closed the door and turned to the police station. He made his way to the double doors and pulled them open. The detectives were just on the other side and leaning against a counter waiting for him.

Money stopped and looked at them.

"This way." One of them said.

Money followed them to the interrogation room. Once inside he took a seat at the table. Both detectives left the room. It was just Money but then the door opened and they came back in. One posted up on the back wall with his hands in his pockets, and the other sat across the table from Money.

"Do you know why you're here?"

"You can at least read me my rights. Right?" Money joked.

"Yep," The detective said then read Money his rights.

"Thank you," Money said. "And yeah I know why I'm here. You told me in the courtroom remember?"

"Yep."

"Murder you said, right?"

"Double homicide actually." The detective corrected. "Better yet, you were there why don't you tell us all about it. The murders that is."

"I don't know shit. You said you wanted to talk, not me." Money said and looked from one to the other.

"You want a sandwich or something?"

"Fuck that sandwich. Not here to make new friends."

"Ok then, shall we start the interview?"

"That's why I'm here right?"

The detective smiled. "Which do you prefer to be called, Money or Ronnie?"

"Ronnie my name ain't it?"

"Okay Ronnie, why don't you tell us about Big World and Lester."

"Y'all the police not me."

"How did you hear about it?"

"You." Money said and stared the detective straight in the eyes.

"After we found their bodies we hit the streets. You probably didn't see it because you were laying low-"

"What's the point?" Money cut him off.

"Your name came up. A lot. Word is that it was you. That you were the last person to see them alive." A smile crossed his lips. "And you've come into some money recently. Want to tell us about that?"

Money dropped his eyes to the tape recorder. He watched how the mechanisms inside spun the tape around. He looked back at the detective then at the other one behind him posted on the wall and shrugged.

"Like you said, I was the last person to see them alive. That means they were alive and not dead. Your own words not mine."

The detective lost his cool and jumped to his feet but his partner stepped up and held him back. He stared at Money. His partner stepped in front of him and took over the conversation.

"Look Money, we know you went to that house with them. We know you knocked his teeth out for the diamonds, and we found your prints all over the house. Help us help you. Talk to us and we can save you from spending the rest of your life inside of a prison cell. We're the only hope you've got." The detective pleaded.

Money was silent with a blank expression on his face.

"Talk to us Money. Come on Ronnie."

Money lifted his head slowly. "I'm guilty."

Both detectives gave Money all of their attention. "You said you're guilty?"

Money nodded.

"Tell us what you're guilty of Ronnie."

Money took a deep breath and looked from one detective to the other then said, "I'm guilty of underage drinking. Look, check this out. Big World was my nigga. The big homie. I would never kill him or anybody. I got scooped up by him, went to the spot over there. Of course you found my prints at the house. Been over there over a hundred times." He stood up.

"Sit down! We're not done with the questions."

Money shook his head no. "Nope, this interview is terminated."

"We can hold you for up to 72 hours."

Money laughed and started for the door. "Ya'll gotta keep in mind that I'm only 15 years old and that ya'll talking to me without an adult present. Don't shit said here tonight mean shit."

One of the detectives pressed the stopped button on the tape recorder and they both watched Money walk out of the room and the door close behind him.

Chapter 9

Outside in the parking lot Money sent Man Man a text and told him that it was time and to get word to the rest of the guys. This was the start of all of their new beginning.

Tae pulled from the parking lot but didn't go straight to Stacy's spot where the meeting was set to be held, instead he pulled in front of a nigga named Banga's house. Banga was known as a gun toting trigger happy ass nigga that with a visit you could get any type of strap you wanted. Tae killed the motor and their eyes bounced around the hood. Niggas in red shirts were everywhere. None of the yards had grass and most of the houses had boards on windows or doors. A shirtless skinny nigga stepped out of the house they were in front of. His body was covered in gang tattoos and a 40 caliber pistol was on his waist.

Money climbed out and nodded at Banga. Banga nodded back then turned and walked inside the house and held the door open for Money. They walked past a woman in a red dress and high heels.

The house was trashed.

They went to the basement. At the mouth of the steps Banga stopped and looked Money in the eyes. "What's good and what you doing around here?"

"I need you. I got some shit jumping off and I need your expertise."

Banga kept his stare locked on Money's eyes. "Why you ain't call before you came? You know how this shit go little nigga."

Money just shrugged. "You got me or not?"

After a brief pause Banga said, "Stay right here," then turned and went deeper in the basement. He came back moments later with a duffel bag, stepped around all the dirty clothes and sat it on top of the dryer and unzipped it. "Check this shit out nigga."

Money looked inside the bag. The first gun his eyes fell on was a .44 magnum. He grabbed it and took aim at the wall. "This what the fuck I'm talking about right here."

"You like that revolver huh?"

"Yeah," Money said and looked at Banga. "They don't leave shit behind at the scene." He smiled and looked at Banga with the Gun in his hands. "Plus dead men tell no tales when they get found unless you tell somebody or leave something. If that shit happen then them dead niggas talk a lot." He held the gun in the air. "How much for this shit right here?"

"Depends on what all you trying to grab."

"Like 10. How much for 10? All revolvers, but I'll take a couple choppers and shotguns too."

Banga massaged his chin in thought. "Give me $2500."

Money paid the man then grabbed the duffel bag and turned for the steps but stopped when Banga called his name. He turned and looked at Banga with the bag in his hands.

"What's good big bro?"

"Be careful out there. I'm only saying this shit because I fuck with you. I heard a couple niggas from Detroit supposed to be on their way down here to collect a ticket on your head."

"It's a ticket on my head?" Money asked with a confused look on his face. Then he smiled.

"Thought you knew. Thought that's why you was down here grabbing all the joints."

"Good looking on the information but it is what it is. It's a cold young world I live in. I'm used to it." He turned and jogged up the steps with the duffel bag, hurried through the house and out to the car where his brother Tae was waiting.

\#

Money got dropped off with the duffel bag over Kendra's house. Everybody was in the living room piled on the couches. There was dope and money on the table. Everybody was there but when Money looked around he didn't see Boo Boo.

"Where Boo Boo at?" He asked the room.

Everyone

"How don't nobody know where this nigga at?"

"He was out here a minute ago. Check the bathroom." Cuz said.

Money turned and walked out the way he came. He stopped at the bathroom door. He pushed it open. It was empty. He continued down the hallway. There were 3 doors besides the bathroom door. He opened the first door. Kids were inside sleeping. At the last door he stopped, pushed it open and stuck his head inside.

Boo Boo jumped up from the bed and hurried to the door and tried to stop Money from entering the room.

"What's up Money? I'm on my way out right now." Boo Boo said and held the door.

"Move from the door," Money said.

Boo Boo didn't move. With all his might Money pushed the door open and knocked Boo Boo to the floor. Money burst in the room stared at the saucer of cocaine on top of the bed. Precious was frozen and just hovered over the plate with wide eyes. she pinched her nostrils closed .

"So this what you in here doing, snorting dope?" Money asked and stared at Boo Boo. He waited for him to say something.

Boo Boo didn't say a word, just picked himself up off the floor and stood in front of Money. "It ain't what it look like."

"What do it look like?" Money asked.

"Look like I was getting high."

"It do don't it?" Money shot back then motioned his head to the bed. "If you ain't getting high then what's that on the bed?"

Boo Boo looked over his shoulder at the dope on the saucer and at the white powder covering Precious's nose. He looked back at Money and shrugged, "I was getting my dick sucked. She was getting high."

Money looked Boo Boo in the eyes then looked at his friend's nose, stared at the white powder hanging from the hairs. "

"Put your shit on and come out here. The meeting about to start."

#

5 minutes later Boo Boo stepped into the living room and all eyes turned to him. Boo Boo pointed forward. "The meeting that way. Fuck y'all looking at me for?"

Everyone turned their eyes back to the front and to Money in front of the TV. There was 15 present.

Okey eyed Boo Boo and said, "Let's start now that everybody here. Everybody come close and make circle around me."

They all made a circle around Money. He eyed everyone. When he got to Boo Boo he saw the white powder under his nose. He closed his eyes and opened them on someone else.

"I've had this vision for over a year now. Everybody know or knew my nigga Blaze. Now he locked up. It was 2 of us on a mission but since he's gone now I see the bigger picture. Why just 2 when we can have hundreds and thousands? I want to start a set where loyalty is everything." He looked at Man Man over his shoulder. "Man Man it's your turn to take the floor." He stepped back, out of the center of the circle, and into the body of the circle.

Man Man stepped forward and into the middle of the circle. "I want everybody to know that when you make an oath that what you put your word on is for life. I might not know everybody here personally but that day will come. If you a part of this family and accept the invitation then touch my hand, and if not, excuse my language but step the fuck out of the circle." Man Man held his hand over his head.

One by one everyone in the circle reached up and touched his hand. When everyone pulled their hand back Man Man pulled out and held up a stack of papers. "What's written on these papers is our laws and policies.

In order for us to be a nation 3 things are required. Law, a flag, and an army to protect what's ours." He stepped out of the circle and brought the duffel bag back inside the circle. He unzipped the duffel bag and pulled it open. Everyone present leaned forward and stared inside the bag at all the guns. "Everybody grab one and pay attention."

Everybody grabbed a gun and examined it. Everyone in the room was armed.

Man Man stood in the middle of the circle with a shotgun and he had their full attention. "This is our nation. We grow it, we protect it, and we live for it."

"We need a name," Cuz said. "A slick ass name."

Money stepped forward. "BPN."

"What it stand for?" Cuz asked.

"Black Pirate Niggas," Money said and held his right hand out to Cuz. Cuz took it and Money guided him through the handshake. "It's easy." He said. "You see the B and the P. We don't do the N."

The rest of them turned to whoever was next to them and extended their hand and they did the handshake. Money went around the room , examined everyone, and did the handshake with everyone with everyone himself. When him and Boo Boo finished Money looked at Boo Boo and said, "You got something white on your nose. You might want to get that together."

Boo Boo wiped the powder off his nose and Man Man pushed past him and walked off. Shine Money. Boo Boo gathered himself and ran behind them both. He caught up with them in the hallway and grabbed Money's arm. "Money wait."

Money turned and faced him with his hand on the knob of the front door. "What's up?"

Boo Boo opened his mouth but no words came out. His mouth just moved a little. He shook his head.

"Just tell me when it started," Money said.

"About 3 months ago. I hit my first line just wanting to fuck longer, but now the shit out of control."

"Why didn't you tell me?"

Boo Boo held up the BPN literature papers. "Because I wanted to be a part of this still. I don't want y'all to look at me different. I need your help Money. Will you help me?"

Money pulled his friend to him and gave him a hug. "Yeah I'll help you," Money said then pulled away and looked him in the eyes, "but you let me down and I'll kill you."

Boo Boo stared at Money the. Buried his face in Money's chest and cried on his shirt.

Money held his friend. "Wipe your face," Money told him. "We gotta go and celebrate the birth of our nation."

Chapter 10

Blaze's sentencing day came fast. The whole process took 3 months. The bailiff walked him out in chains and stood him in front of the podium. He looked at the judge.

In the pews Alicia stood up and rubbed her stomach. "I love you."

The chatter in the courtroom stopped and everyone turned and stared at Alicia. They turned back when the bailiff got everyone's attention.

"Everyone rise for the honorable Judge Mackey."

The entire front row was filled with people wearing 'free Blaze' t – shirts.

The judge walked in and sat at his bench. He looked down at Blaze like he was the lowest thing he had ever seen the. opened Blaze's file, read some then looked up at Blaze again and went into a long speech, "As a judge I'm compelled to tell you that you're a part of the problem. The youth these days, especially in urban communities are terrorizing society..." he gave a long spiel then cleared his throat when he finished.

"Do you know why you're here, in this courtroom, and in front of me today?"

Blaze nodded. "Yes sir, I do."

"To be 16 years old you have an extensive record. Do you understand that?"

"Sir I-"

The judge cut him off. "It's a yes or no question."

Blaze nodded.

"Very good. I hereby sentence you for the possession of crack cocaine, with intent to sale or manufacture less than 50 grams. The term of sentence shall be served at the Glenn Mills Boys Training school." The judge bent over his bench and peered deep into Blaze's soul. "The length of the sentence shall depend on how long it takes you to get your G.E.D. , and however long it takes you to complete the other recommendations the staff at the training school may think you need. This will teach you responsibility. The choice is yours how much time you will do."

The 2 bailiffs walked Blaze out of the courtroom with Alicia at hung and holding her stomach. In the hallway people lined the wall. They were all from the free world. Blaze felt like a sideshow at the circus.

Money, Alicia and Tricia walked out of the courtroom just in time to see him waddle around a corner of the corner with jail guards and out of sight.

Chapter 11

Right after Blaze's sentencing Money went and got his little brother
and sister from their father's crib. They were both doomed with a junky
for a mother. He had money coming in, could afford to take care of them,
and keep them with him unlike before. Now he had the means, and would
use them. Ok then to Tricia's house but told them the next day he would
go and see about a new house for them all.

#

The next day Money went to see a white man named Jared. Jared
helped him get a house, and did it all I. A single day.

When they made it back to Jared's office from viewing the house
Money asked him about things that made money outside of drugs. Money
had a clothing store on his mind ,but when he brought that up to Jared the
things Jared said made him see things from a completely different angle.

"A clothing store is cool," Jared said, "but that shit don't exactly make
money by itself. You need something that you have to just put out there
once and people spend their money, not something you gotta keep being

creative to generate a dollar. That defeats the purpose of creating a passive income."

Money stared at Jared. "Whatever," he told him. "This your world. Just get me together. I got faith in you."

Outside of all the real estate Jared had he also owned car lots. Not just one but a few, and not just bullshit cars but expensive shit. Shit that dope boys dreamed about.

"The nightclub business is where it's at," Jared told Money. "The money that flows through it is crazy. The door, liquor, raffles, literally o one can count your money. And the tax write offs that comes with it! Awesome."

"Yeah?" Was all a Money could get out. He was amazed.

"That's where you need to put your money," Jared said. "One hundred percent guarantee that at your level that's the best place for your cash. Talk to yo brother about it and get back to me."

#

Money left Jared's office and picked up Tricia and took her out to eat at a fancy restaurant and ran the idea of club ownership by her. And when they left he took her to their new house blindfolded. When he took the blindfold off he popped a bottle as she stared and gawked at her née house.

\#

Later that day Money went back to Jared's office. Jared took Money to look at a few buildings that could be turned into clubs. It only took Money to see the 2 buildings before he made his choice. As soon as they walked inside and Money looked at the architecture he knew he had found the place.

"This is it right here," he said and turned to Jared. "I don't need to view anymore spaces. This is it!"

They took a bunch of pictures and Jared dropped him off at his car. When Money got out. Jared lowered his window and said, "Stop by my office later and we can fill out the paper work. Probably interview some strippers while we're at it," he laughed.

Money nodded and watched Jared pull off with a wide smile on his face then jumped in his car and went home.

#

He walked in the house and took off his shoes at the door. Tricia was on the couch, just staring at him with a sour face.

"What's wrong with you, why your face all fucked up?" He asked her.

"I'm worried about us," She told him

He sat next to her on the couch. She stared at him for a moment longer then laid her head on his chest. He could feel her breath on his neck.

"What you worried about?" He asked her.

"The future," She said, then, "Plus I think I'm pregnant Money."

Money stiffened under her.

"You mad?" She asked.

"Mad about what? You sound crazy. Why you just now telling me? And how long?"

She laughed lightly. "Maybe 3 weeks and I didn't tell you because I was scared and I didn't know how you would react. I already gotta tell my mom." She kissed his lips. "I always think about what if something happens to you too. What will I do? What will me and he baby do?"

He kissed her back. "Nothing's going to happen to me," he promised her. "I'm out here getting shit in order so that no matter what you'll be taken care of."

"I don't like living like this Money."

"I know," he exhaled. "Me neither. It won't be too much longer though."

"Promise?" She asked.

"I promise." He hugged her hard.

Chapter 12

Money stopped out by the mall at a jewelry store. Like most of the jewelry stores it was owned by an Arab. The pieces inside were nice but that wasn't why Money was there. He approached the counter and the clerk smiled at him. He was a big heavy set Arab with a mouth filled with gold teeth.

"How may I help you?" The words rolled off the man's tongue poetically.

Money dug in his pocket and came out with a velvet sack. He set it on the glass countertop. "I need something madeA special piece. Something custom and dope as fuck."

The jeweler picked up the velvet sack, loosened the string, then poured the contents on the glass. Big World's colorful rainbow teeth gleamed in the light on the countertop. The jeweler looked up at Money then casually scooped the jeweled teeth back inside the bag. He looked around and slid the bag in his back pocket and cleared his throat. "And what am I to do with these?"

Money opened his phone and showed the jeweler a necklace. "I want them turned into this."

The jeweler stared at the necklace in the photo then into Money's eyes. His stare was cold. "When do you want the piece?"

"In 2 weeks for my birthday party."

The jeweler nodded and Money laid a wad of cash of the counter then turned and started for the door.

chapter 13

2 weeks later money went to the jewelry store to pick up the necklace. When the jeweler brought the necklace out from the back Money smiled from ear to ear when he saw it.

"Something like this?" The jeweler asked but knew from the look in Money's eyes that he had hit the nail right on the head with the colorful piece.

Money grabbed the necklace and held it up. "It's exactly what I wanted." He put the necklace on then turned to the others so they could see how it looked on him. "How this shit look?"

"That shit fit you. This your world Money." Youngin said.

Cuz rushed inside the jewelry store. Everyone turned and looked at him. "Just got a call from Man Man. He said some Detroit niggas got Kendra's house surrounded."

Everyone hurried outside and into the cars waiting outside.

Inside the car the driver punched it and Money stared at Cuz. "Run it back from the beginning," Money listened Closely then asked, "How you know they from Detroit?"

"That's what Man Man said. It was all he said, said some Detroit niggas was outside with their straps out and using their cars for shields."

Money and the driver locked eyes in the rearview mirror. "Smash it to Kendra spot."

Everyone inside the car braced themselves as the car accelerated and weaved in and out of traffic barely missing cars and trucks.

#

At the mouth of Kendra's alley the cars filled with BPN members skidded into the alley, shut off the lights of the car, and eased down the bumpy alley. He stopped 2 houses down from Kendra's and they climbed out, drew their guns and snuck up to Kendra's house.

They jumped out and ran inside Kendra's house. They searched the house but found nothing. After seeing it was empty they reassembled in the kitchen, all of them with their guns out.

"Nothing here," Cuz said.

"I know," Money said with his 357 Magnum in his hand, "but the front door wide open. They got him. I know they do. Why the fuck else he ain't here with us?"

A phone rung, but it was none of the BPN member's phones, but a phone sitting on the counter. Money walked over and grabbed it. It was a 313 number calling. Money answered it.

"Yo," was all he said and listened. He turned back to his brothers, motioned with his eyes to the phone and looked out of the window. He looked up at the streetlights. They were all shot out when they hadn't been shot out before.

Money studied every car and every house with the 357 in his hand and the phone to his ear . "We ain't gotta do all the talking. Who is this?"

Laughter came through earpiece. A sinister and evil laugh. "I know what happened to Big World, and if you want to see this bitch ass nigga alive again put whoever that nigga named Money is on the phone."

"This is Money. What's up?"

"Damn homie, why you knock my man's teeth out like that? He gone," the voice on the phone said, "but he ain't forgotten pussy."

Money disregarded everything then said, "let me speak to Man Man."

"Your days of calling shots over with. Just wait until I catch up with you and pull your teeth out." The laughter came again. This time more sinister, and crazier.

"Who is you?" Money asked.

"It don't matter who I am, just meet me at Muskegon High School at 2 AM. You don't show up I'm offing this nigga anyway, and then I'm coming to find and off you too." The phone went dead.

"What was in the front?" Cuz asked.

"Nothing but she'll casings and they shot out the lights." Money looked out the windows again. "We gotta go."

As soon as they walked out the backdoor they ran into Boo Boo and stopped in their tracks. Sirens were in the distance. They all took their eyes off Boo Boo and looked in the direction the sirens were coming from. People started coming outside around the neighborhood. Money looked back at Boo Boo. He knew Boo Boo hadn't been with them before. Boo Boo looked at Money too.

"Where you come from?" Money asked and looked him up and down. His clothes were on his body awkwardly and again he had the white powder under his nose. "You walked here?"

Boo Boo shook his head. "Nope, I parked down the street."

The sirens were close and getting closer. Money looked off in the distance. "Ok. We gotta go. Police on their way."

They all piled into their cars and fled the scene just as the cops turned onto Kendra's block.

#

A few hours later at the spot Money and the gang sat around the table and stared at one another in silence. The only thing they did do was watch the clock, and at 1:30 AM Money stood up. "Let's go and set up early, see what we can catch."

#

On the way to the football field Cuz, who was behind the wheel driving looked over at Money and asked, "Why you think these niggas want to meet at the high school? Shit don't really make no sense to me."

"Because the lights are always on at the school and plus there's a lot of room."

When they pulled up to the school they saw a pair of dudes struggling to get another man inside of the fence. They watched for a moment then jumped out of he car. Then with their guns drawn they made their way to the fence and followed the men inside.

The corridor was long, wide, and hollow.

Just inside they saw gang of men a ways down and called out to them. They turned with their revolvers on the ready. Even though they were shadows it was easy to see that they had someone with them, and that they were holding them at gunpoint.

It had to be Man Man. They stopped at one of the doors, opened it and went trigger fingers ready they went inside.

Money and the others crept up to the door then stopped. Money looked, and while he was looking the doorknob began to twist. The BPN members all hurried away from the door and around the corner and out of sight. A man stepped out. He had a gun in his hand.

"I left it in the car, I'll be right back," the man said and closed the door. With his gun in his hand he started down the hallway.

He went in the opposite direction.

When the dude was a ways down Money jumped out from the corner and ran after the man. At the sound of the foot steps the man turned. Even though startled he went to raise his gun but Money clotheslined him at the neck. The man dropped to the ground hard and hit his head on the cement floor. The gun slid from his hand.

Money pulled him around the corner where the others were, then him and Cuz stepped out with guns drawn and knocked on the door. When it opened Money put his gun to the man's temple and said, "Open the door all the way, and don't say shit."

He snatched the man's gun from his hand and stepped in. He took the gun from the man's temple and shot him in the chest, then he turned and shot the last man standing that was standing over Man Man with his gun out. 2 shots under his armpit dropped him quick.

Money ran over and untied Man Man. Once free Man Man pushed the dead man off of him and grabbed the his gun.

Every BON member present stood over the last man shot. Blood gurgled from his mouth and the look in his eyes were of pity. The BPN members unloaded their guns into the his body then ran from the room, hurried down the stadium hallways, and back out to the truck where Kendra was behind the wheel waiting for them. They slammed the doors and Kendra fumbled to get the gear in drive, but when she did the car peeled out from the high school.

Chapter 14

Back on Amity street at Kendra's spot everybody hugged and showed loved to everyone had came out alive and not just Man Man. Money gave the 357 and Blaze's gun to Kendra to put up, then met her in her bedroom and closed the door behind him.

"I need the other guns," he told her when the door was closed.

Kendra went to the closet and pulled out the duffel bag and gave it to Money. He dug inside and came out with 2 revolvers, stuffed them on his waist and looked at Kendra. "Get rid of the 2 I just gave you, and make sure to watch your phone and the back door. I'll be back."

He exited and went to the living room.

Money stared at everyone. He had the revolver out and in his hand. He said no words because no words needed to be said. Instead he turned, opened the door, then turned back to his gang. One by one they walked past Money and exited Kendra's house. Paper was the last man to walk past. Money reached out and grabbed him. Paper turned and stared at Money. Money held out the the other gun to him.

"From this point on," he said, "You're my right hand. My eyes and ears. My mouth when I ain't around."

They exited together and Money closed the door behind them.

Chapter 15

The BPN niggas were in 2 cars and strapped to the teeth. Money, Paper, and 2 more BPN members were in the lead car, and they were bent corner after corner in search of the rest of the Detroit niggas.

"Everybody be on the lookout." Money said with the revolver in his hand. He looked in the backseat at another member with an AK – 47 laid across his lap. "These niggas still up here."

"How the fuck you know?"

"Everybody know Detroit niggas don't go nowhere 1 car deep."

The car moved through the night streets with grace. It moved at a slow speed as the men's eyes inside searched and scanned both sides of the street. Every abandoned house, empty lot, and abandoned building. Every tall blade of grass, because like tigers some liked to stalk and sneak. But they saw nothing, the streets were dead. Virtually no cars were out. No one was on the corners, and nobody were at any of the stores.

A police car sat on almost every corner. The streets were hot after all the recent crime that had crushed it. The gangs were growing. Recruits were getting younger and members were growing older, which meant they weren't dropping out, retiring, and were standing on the foundations of gang culture.

"When we find these niggas," Money said and looked around the car at each person's face, "every last one of these niggas gotta go."

After another hour of riding and searching the city they came to a red light at a busy street. "Pull over and let's get something to eat."

Paper pulled into the lot of J Burger and Wings. The parking lot was packed. But it was one vehicle that stuck out to Money. A solid black F250. Paper slammed on the breaks in front of the truck. There were 2 passengers inside and they both looked up from their trays of food and when they saw the car filled with BPN members their eyes got big.

Money raised his revolver and Paper snatched the AK – 47 from the lap of the sleeping member in the backseat, let the window down and hopped on the windowsill. He took aim over the hood of the car and at the same time both Money and Paper opened fire.

Both men in the front seat of the truck dropped their trays, opened their doors, and tried to jump out, but were both too slow. Bullets cut them down and ate up the front of the truck including both open doors.

The bystanders parked around the truck in the lot jumped out and ran screaming while some sped off in their cars hitting other vehicles as they went.

The shooting stopped and the 2 men that had been in the front were hanging out of the open doors of the truck. Blood dripped from the wholes in their bodies. But they were still moving. Money opened his door and got out, Paper did too. They split up at the hood of the truck and each went to a different door.

The members in the other car piled out too and stood watch in all directions to make sure that whoever came from whichever way would be sure to meet certain death.

Money and Paper opened fire. This time they made sure their prey was dead before they lowered their guns. They looked at the men they had just slain.

"Boo Boo," Money called out.

Boo Boo ran up to Money's side. "What up Money?"

"Check them nigga's pockets."

"Man fuck them niggas Money they dead."

"Check them nigga's pocket like I said." This time authority was in Money's voice. "This ain't me asking Boo Boo, this me telling you.

With his gun in hand Boo Boo walked toward the bullet riddled truck. He made it 2 steps before Money and Paper opened fire. Boo Boo was cut to pieces from the back.

Money and Paper, both with smoking guns, stepped backwards to the car, got in and closed their doors. The other car filled with BPN members trailed them as they fled the scene and dodged and maneuvered through the fleeing bystanders and onlookers on the scene.

Chapter 16

Money had all but disappeared on Tricia, but even as a young nigga he knew that keeping those that could hurt him closest to him was the best thing to do. After smoking the Detroit niggas Money decided it would be best to lay low, but not with Tricia but with Kendra.

That didn't last long though. Just 3 days into laying low he was ready to go. He had barely slept since the murders, he just sat in a chair in the motel room and watched Kendra nod on the bed and dip in and out of the bathroom. He looked at her sleeping on the bed one last time. He knew he had to get away from her. He got up and like she was some cheap hooker he left her in the motel room and went home. He would just take his chances.

#

At home he walked through the door cautiously. He hadn't seen or talked to Tricia in days. Tricia must have heard him come through the door because she walked into the living room with her robe on. Tricia was mature for her age. Being Money's other half had done that to her. Had seasoned her, worn her, but also had made her smarter. It was a good trade off. She didn't say a word just stared at him then turned and went back

into their bedroom.

Chapter 17

"Happy 17th birthday," the d.j. shouted into the microphone loud enough so his voice could be carried over the music. "To the man of the day, Young Money." The entire club erupted in shouts and cheers. "And to many more."

A year passed like the blink of the eye. Even though he had what many viewed as a small army, Money still felt empty without Blaze.

Tricia leaned over and kissed Money then got to her feet and her and Alicia walked out of the V.I.P. booth. When they were all the way out of sight Paper held up a bottle of Hennessy.

"A toast," Paper said.

Money held up a bottle of Remy Martin and repeated after Paper, "A toast."

"To the flyest, coldest young nigga I know. To my nigga Money. Happy birthday."

They clanked the bottles together and turned them up at the same time. Tricia and Alicia came back into the booth with a giant cake decorated with sparklers and candles. It was so big they had to hold it with both hands. They held it in front of Money.

"Make a wish and blow out your candles baby," Tricia told him excitedly.

Money stood up, closed his eyes, made a wish, and blew out the candles with a smile on his face. Right on cue the club's cameraman stepped in the booth and snapped pictures.

Money saw Kendra moving fast through the crowd. He put his lips to Tricia's ear. "I'll be right back."\

He kissed her cheek and slid off. He caught up with Kendra fast and grabbed her by the shoulder, spun her around to him. They were face to face. "What you doing here?" Money asked her.

"Partying," She said and sucked her teeth. "You disappeared on me and then ask me what I'm doing in a club a year later." She laughed and started back toward the inside of the club. "Nigga fuck you. Let me go and holla at your bitch real quick. See do she know you hunting other bitches down in the club."

Money grabbed her again and snatched her to him. It was obvious she was drunk. He put one of his arms around her neck and walked her to the side door of the club. He didn't want to make a scene but had already drawn attention.

Outside and on the side of the club in the parking lot Money and Kendra just stared at one another.

"So now what?" Money asked her.

"I love you Money." Her tone was hushed. Really low. She was embarrassed but didn't care. "I love you. Why can't you see that I can be everything you need?" Tears poured from her eyes. She took a step towards him. "Just give me another chance. You don't need her."

When he didn't respond she punched him in the chest repeatedly.

To stop her assault Money grabbed her and snatched her into a hug. He put his lips to her ear. "It's over Kendra. I only love Tricia and you know that."

Tricia stepped out of the club's side door and saw Money hugging Tricia. Money looked over and saw Tricia standing in the parking lot just 2 feet away watching him hug another woman. The look on her face was priceless. Money didn't say a word just let Kendra go, looked her in the eyes and said, "That's why right there."

He palmed her face with his right hand and pushed her as hard as he could. She flew backwards, then fell on the ground. She was motionless and on her stomach with her hair and clothes in disarray. She looked up at Money. "Please," She begged.

Money walked over, wrapped an arm around Tricia. They headed for the club's side door but were stopped by in their tracks by the 2 detectives in front of them. Money removed his hand from around Tricia then turned and faced the detectives. "What the fuck you niggas want?"

"I think you know what the fuck we niggas want," one of the detectives said then laughed at his own joke. "We want to know what's up with you and the cats that came up here from Detroit? Your name ringing real loud bells out here in he streets Young Money, or should I call you Young World?"

Money turned to Tricia. "Go wait for me in the car baby," he told her, then watched her until she climbed in the car. He stepped closer to the detectives. "I don't know why ya'll keep fucking with me, but for all I can see, it look like don't nobody like them niggas. I can't help that and I ain't got shit to do with it. They must have rubbed somebody the wrong way," he said then opened his car door and climbed halfway inside but stopped and looked at the cops. "I gotta dip though. I would love to stay and kick it, but unlike ya'll I got other shit to do besides sitting here wasting time."

Both detectives smiled as Money climbed in the car. "Sure," one of them said. "We'll see you later."

Chapter 18

Meetings were a weekly thing for the BPN members, but they knew that the meeting Money had called unexpectedly was strange. Everyone knew something was up. It had already been explained and understood that there would be penalties for those that weren't at the meeting. Or those that were even late. Even though majority of them were young boys and young men, none of them acted like it, and if they did their behavior would be corrected quickly, and they would be dealt with.

Money cleared his throat. All eyes went front and center to him. "What's good and how the brother's doing?" He waited while the crowd all at once told him how they were doing, then he continued. "We have meetings all the time, but this meeting is different. Today I want to talk about territory, money, and how depending on how we look at the 2 they can be the same thing, or they can be opposites. But for us and for the purposes of this meeting today, our view is a connected view, where territory, space, and location all mean money."

He eyed the members in the room, there were a lot of new faces and young faces. He took a deep breath, starting a gang was a huge task, but expanding and growing that same gang was an even bigger task and Money knew it. But though no matter how big he was still up for the task.

"Everybody familiar with the project housing units in this room right?" He waited and watched as everyone nodded their heads. "Good, then everybody should be glad to know that the projects is the target and that means everybody should know that the projects only got 2 entrances and 2 exits. There's only 2 ways in and 2 ways out." A smile as wide as the Mississippi river spread across Money's lips.

"Genius huh?" Man Man stepped forward and asked. "With tightly controlled entrances and exits we can channel all the traffic to the projects, control everything that comes in and out, even the police. Recruit everybody inside the projects. So many safe houses we won't ever be able to count them all.

Money spoke up. "So again like at the first meeting whoever ain't with the shit we on they can dip, with no repercussions. All you gotta do is get up and walk out the door right now and that's your right. But if you don't get up and walk out the door right now, then we locked in and ain't no turning back. Ain't no turning down orders, ain't no turning your Back on the brothers or the mob. None of that shit." He stared at everybody but again no one said a word. He scanned the membership, his eyes fell on a young member that he had never saw before and pointed to him. "What's your name?"

"Cutter," the young member told him.

"Cutter do you know what you getting into? What we about to do? We're about to go on a campaign that will give us total control. We will run shit. This is for power and territory. It might get bloody. Wars might be started behind this shit. Lives might be lost. And freedoms."

Cutter stood from the chair and kept his attention front and center. He swallowed hard. "I do," Cutter said.

"You from the projects ain't you?"

Cutter nodded. "I am."

"Good. The takeover starts tomorrow. I want a complete takeover. Everything. Anybody say anything against what we doing, then everybody got the green light to handle that shit however they see fit. Most importantly we need to go in their and set an example from the jump."

Chapter 19

North gate

The BPN members surrounded the projects. They split into 2 groups and were just outside of both entrances. They had the projects completely cut off. People came out of their units and stared at the gang members just outside the fence that was supposed to protect their homes and where they lived. Every BPN member had on bulletproof vests and guns. They looked like real soldiers how they stood next to the vehicles they'd come in and smoked blunts and passed bottles back and forth.

#   #   #

South Gate

At the south gate BPN members were also assembled and smoking blunts and passing bottles with their bulletproof vests and guns just like the others were at the North Gate. There was one difference at this gate though, and the people noticed. There was one man that wasn't smoking and passing blunts and bottles like the others. Instead he was staring at the projects and the people that came out of them with so much focus one could have thought he was a mannequin. It was Money and he was focused. He knew the importance of what he was about to do. He knew that if he pulled it off that he would solely shape the future of the city. The culture of all of the gangs that came and went. Everything would be in his control. It would be his legacy.

This was the most important fight of his life. He knew this was an all out battle, and not just for the projects, but for the entire city. He knew that if the projects fell, then so would the rest of the city because the projects were one of the only hoods within the city that had a strong sense of hood pride, whereas every other hood was just running around and were basically renegades, a gang society with no identity.

Money watched as the project niggas that were expected to do the fighting and defending started popping out of units and from behind units with hoodies on. They formed a small crowd and watched the scene and the gang members continue to pile up outside the project gates. Money turned and got his membership's attention. They all turned his way, with the blunts and bottles in hand. Money didn't say a word, just turned back to the projects with his gun in his hand and watched as more and more project niggas piled out of the units and into yards with guns in their hands.

For years the project niggas had defended their territory fiercely. But even though the projects had a tight knit community the had no structure, and that's exactly what was the driving force behind Money's plan. They had governed themselves and had kept out everyone and from entering their domain. They knew the landscape and could wage guerrilla warfare better than anyone, and they were ready. Maybe not as organized as the BPN niggas, but they were ready.

Money pulled a walkie talkie to his lips. "When I give the word we attack from both sides."

#   #   #

At the other gate Paper pulled the walkie talkie from his ear and put it to his mouth. "Copy that, ready whenever you give the word."

He removed the walkie talkie from his lips and looked up at the projects. But now they were empty and not one single person was outside or visible like just a moment before.

#

Money moved the walkie talkie from his ear and looked at the project niggas less than 100 feet away from him. A big man in the front, and with a shotgun held up his left hand and signaled to his people, and like trained soldiers they all stepped backwards and disappeared in the darkness like they had never been there at all.

Money put the walkie talkie back to his lips and held up his left hand at the same time. He gave the signal to both the membership behind him and the membership on the walkie talkie and posted up at the other gate.

"Attack!" He shouted into the walkie talkie and pointed forward with the free hand and all of the BPN niggas behind him rushed forward, through the fence, and into the dusty project courtyard with guns blazing.

The BPN members stopped in their tracks as the project niggas jumped out of their hiding places. They were on rooftops with rifles pointed at the BPN members, and some had lit Molotov cocktails in their hands.

A big man on the roof screamed like a crazed warrior and opened fire at the BON members with an AK – 47.

Then all hell broke loose.

The BPN members tried to take aim but were too slow.s

On the rooftops from the open or broken and shot out project windows the project niggas opened fire.

#

Out in the courtyard the bullets made impact as they burrowed into BPN members and swept them off their feet. The ones that didn't get hit by bullets looked down at their fallen, then put their attention back tot the fight in front of them. The fight for their homeland and kept firing. The project niggas on the ground kept pushing forward and aiming at anything not from the projects.

#

The scene was the same at the other gate.

The BPN members crossed the threshold into the back courtyard and the fighting was cut off from the public eye.

Project niggas jumped out of dumpsters and from behind crumbling brick walls and made the best attack on BPN members hey possibly could.

There were too many BPN members, and even more important, they all had a goal and a common purpose plus the elect of surprise.

The last sniper on the roof got shot in the center of his chest and fell to the ground. The protection their fire the snipers provided were gone.

The BPN members overran the project and it only took less than 5 minutes. They encircled the remaining and standing project niggas in the middle of the courtyard. They backpedaled until their backs touched one another in a small circle they formed. They still had their guns in their hands but to shoot would have been a complete suicide mission. But they had nowhere to go.

Money stepped forward with his gun up. The other BPN members did too. They were right behind Money. "Drop them guns, or get gunned down right here. All we want is the projects, not y'all. Give us what we came for, or die."

The lead project nigga that had been on the roof was bunched in the circle and covered with blood. The shotgun was still in his hand, but now he was covered in blood and favoring his right side. He looked down at the shotgun in his bloody hand then up at Money. He looked down the barrel of Money's gun then bent and laid the shotgun on the cement then put his hands up in surrender . The others in the kill zone the same. Put their guns down and threw their hands up.

"Take 'em, their yours," the leader said.

"Good decision," Money told him then turned to his soldiers. "See who want to convert, and see who don't. We'll go from their. These projects belong to BPN."

Man Man went around to the men that had surrendered with a piece of paper and pen and asked if they were converting to BPN, if he marked them down, and if not they got smacked across the head with the pistol, kicked in the ass and sent off with a stern message to stay out of the projects. The BPN members jumped in their cars, burned rubber doin u turns then formed a line and exited the projects in fashion knowing they had sent a clear message and gained an important piece of geography.

Money and Paper ended up in the same car. Money looked at Paper. At 17 Money was the most powerful person in the city. The last stronghold in the city had surrendered and converted and those that didn't were exiled or destroyed.

"In a minute I plan on disappearing," Money said out of the blue on the way to the safe house.

Paper looked at him but said nothing.

Money continued. "Just know that whenever I do make the decision I want you to come with me. Just fade out. fade to black."

Chapter 20

3 months later

One of the Black Pirates was in a project stairwell getting his dick sucked by a dope fiend. His pants were halfway down, and the fiend was in between his legs and going to town for the crack he was paying her. He snatched her head up when she bit him. With a handful of her hair in one hand he slapped her across the face with the other hand. "Bitch don't you ever bite me hoe."

2 BPN members opened the stairwell door and walked in. They stopped and stared at the member and then the fiend. The member got to his feet, looked over his shoulder and saw them then turned back to the fiend.

"Get your dope fiend ass out of here before I kick you down the stairs bitch."

When the fiend exited through the thick metal door one of the 2 turned to the young members. "You in here getting your dick sucked? Major violation."

The other member laughed. "But all bullshit aside, you don't even know who that fiend was do you?"

The young member shook his head no.

"That's Kendra, Money's old bitch. She gets high now. We ain't gone say shit about you getting your little duck sucked but keep that shit in your pants and get your shit together."

All 3 of them stepped outside. They stared at Kendra across the parking lot at one of their rock apartments. She gave the man her money at the door. He turned away and while she waited she was antsy. She looked over her shoulder and saw them watching.

The server came back to the window and gave her the rock. She tucked it in her bra, tucked her head, and disappeared around the unit and out of their sight.

All 3 of them shook their heads.

"That's sad."

"That's reality nigga. You niggas better get with this shit or y'all gon' have a lot of fucked up experiences."

"Should we tell Money?" One of them asked.

"When the time comes we will, but until then, fuck that bitch."

Chapter 21

The baby made Blaze feel like he had never felt before when he laid eyes on him. Seeing his son in person was different than looking at him in the pictures that Alicia had sent him to the lock up. He felt weird knowing that he had created life. Even deeper responsibility.

Blaze held his baby while the others watched. Hugged him for 20 minutes straight. It was his first home visit and he wanted to hold and spend as much time with his son as he could, as well as the rest of his friends and family.

Money walked in and fucked up the entire vibe. "I need you to run and shoot this move with us real quick Blaze."

Blaze stared at him with the baby in his arms. Alicia and Tricia looked at him too. No one present could believe that he was asking Blaze to ride on gang business while he was on a home visit. Money didn't dodge the stares, instead he matched them. Absorbed them.

After waging the bloody campaign to take the projects, and ultimately the city since Money had BPN seize majority of the city that was easy to take with minimum force, Money had even gained interest in the down town area where most of the legal weed licensees were issued. Expansion was his driving by force. Growing BPN into an all out army and powerhouse with legitimate businesses was starting to run through his mind. The possibilities were endless and he didn't give a fuck what he had to do to accomplish his goals.

"Okay," Blaze told him and handed the baby off to Alicia and followed Money and Paper out the door looking at Alicia and his child over his shoulder the entire time. They climbed in the car. Money pulled a 45 from his waist and laid it across his lap. And the car pulled into traffic. "Where we going?" Blaze asked. Paper looked at the gun then up into Money 's eyes.

"Nation business. Everything good my nigga." Money said and right then and there he realized the power he actually had, which was a lot,.

Money turned an eye to Blaze and eyed him back. Money's appearance had fell since the project takeover. The time since he had spent drinking and pacing the basement floor in the dark and moonlight.

"It's good to be home," Blaze told Money. It was their first exchange besides the order to take the ride. "Good to see everybody too."

"Yeah, shit crazy out here. We need all the help we can get. Glad you here too." He went in the glovebox and gave held out a small pistol to Blaze.

"Who is we?" Blaze asked.

"BPN," Money said. "The nation we built." Money still had the gun held out.

Blaze stared at it for a moment, then as if in slow motion he reached out and grabbed it, brought it across his lap and looked at it. It was then and there that he knew shit was different and would never be the same.

Money drove off. A few blocks into the drive he looked at Blaze and casually said, "I had to drop Boo Boo. He was out of pocket." He shook his head. "It's so much shit that's been going on out here. Glad I can bring you up to speed on everything. I missed you."

#

They pulled into a car dealership. It belonged to Jared, the same white realtor that had found Money his house, and the business shit he had set up for organization.

They were escorted in and led to an office in the back where they could meet in private and discuss their business. Jared took a seat in the chair behind his desk and relaxed, kicked his feet up. "Money, my main man, how's the house treating you?"

"Everything's good." Money said and sat down. "Tricia and my siblings love it. Couldn't ask for a better spot, or a better realtor. But I'm here to chop it up with you about some other shit."

Jared held a hand up and cut Money off. He pointed to the phone on his desk. "I don't do business around technology or with or in front of strangers." He looked past Money at Blaze. "No disrespect but I don't know this guy you dragged in here with you."

Money looked at Blaze. "This my homie Blaze. Been down in Philly."

"Still," Jared maintained.

Blaze, with his eyes locked on Jared got to his feet. He turned slowly and exited the office and closed the door behind him. When the door was closed Money turned back to Jared behind the desk.

"You don't trust me huh?"

"Nothing personal, just business," Jared said. "Now what was it that you wanted to talk to me about again?"

"Heroin," Money told him.

Jared's face turned beat red. He loosened his tie and fidgeted in his seat.

Money continued. "I got 2 hundred thousand dollars I want to spend. All cash. Can you make it happen?"iq

Jared regained his composure and his face regained its color too. He leaned forward in the office chair and across his desk. "Your other business not doing much for you?" He asked then relaxed in the seat. "Never mind. I can do it but I don't need money. I'll get you what you want, but I need you to help me with a little problem I haven't been able to have taken care of."

Money looked at Paper then back to Jared across the desk. "Just tell me what you need?"

Jared smiled. It was a devilish smile. He leaned across the desk again. Closer to Money. "There's a store I need you to visit," he told Money. "It's on the corner of Amity and Fork. The guy inside sales urban clothing. His name is Malcom." He looked into Money's eyes. He didn't say what he wanted, just nodded when Money locked his stare.

Money back then him and Blaze got to their feet. "We'll be back to see you in a day or 2. Be on the look out for us."

They exited the office.

Blaze was standing in the middle of the hallway with hatred on his face. It was obvious how he felt. Back in the car he could hardly hold back his disdain for what Money, his childhood friend and brother had turned into. It was clear to see that Money was not the same person he remembered. He had made a lot of moves since he'd killed Big World and Lester, but at what cost? One thing was obvious from Blaze's in person observation, and that was Money was making everything sound better than it actually was.

#

They pulled up to the project's south gate and they were confronted by BPN security. 2 BPN members with guns out walked up to the car, looked inside, then stepped away when they saw who it was and let the car pass through the gate.

Blaze stared in awe and was shocked at the organization and the traffic. The way everyone wielded guns out in the open, and sold drugs like it was legal was beyond him. A lot had changed since he'd been gone. They gave him a short tour of he project complex, then pulled up to the main building, parked and got out.

Only the original members really knew who Blaze was, the rest of the membership only knew of his legend and who he was to Money. The day he got locked up was wrapped in with the myth of their gang's creation. That meant Blaze was important.

They walked into a unit used for members to chill on their breaks. When they walked in all the members present stood rigid and at full attention. Guns were everywhere. So was drugs, scales, and money.

Knew addressed the room. "For all the brothers that don't know who this is, this is Blaze, the big homie that's been locked up in Philly. Show him some love."

One by one the membership walked up and shook Blaze's hand. Showed him some love BPN style.

The 2 members that had caught the little nigga getting his dick sucked in the stairwell walked in. They scanned the room and saw him and he panicked. The little nigga that had been getting his dick sucked stepped backwards in the crowd, and eased to the backwards. He bumped everybody as he went.

One of them to whispered in Money's ear but kept his eyes on the young nigga. Money's eyes went to the young dude too.

The little nigga broke into a sprint. He pushed through the crowd and tried for the door but was grabbed by 3 BPN members from the crowd.

Money walked up in the little nigga's face. Everyone formed a circle around them.

"What you running for?" Money asked him.

Money didn't wait for an answer. He punched him in the neck and then the nose. Blood poured from his nose. Money yanked a gun from his pants and put it to the young dude's head.

"You like disrespecting niggas in the organization?" Money asked and pulled the hammer back on the revolver.

A hand reached out and grabbed the gun.

Money looked over his shoulder to see who it was that had grabbed him. It was Blaze. He moved the gun from the young dude's face, turned, and put the gun to Blaze's cheek.

Blaze slowly extended his hands out toward Money. "It's me Money, Blaze. Your brother, Paul, brothers since the sand box. Think about it. Look at ,e. See who I am."

The two friends locked eyes.

Money broke the stare. "Don't you ever grab me again in your life nigga," he said and a tear rolled down his face, but he kept his finger on the trigger.

2 members stepped next to Blaze and were ready to grab him just in case he ran. To the, he was a completes stranger.

Paper stepped up to Money's side and put a hand on his shoulder. "That's Blaze Money, your brother."

With trembling lips Money looked at Paper, then slowly he lowered the gun. When the gun was off him Blaze snatched Money into a hug and Paper grabbed the gun from Money's hand and set it to the side.

The two friends would never be the same again.

#

On the way to drop Blaze off Money rode in silence. Blaze and Paper were did. The only noise came from the speakers. They parked in front of Blaze's spot and Money and Blaze looked at one another in the dark car on the dark street. Childhood friends since birth knew they were at a crossroad in their friendship.

"A lot of shit done changed around here if you can't tell," Money told him in the darkness. "You done got soft my nigga."

Blaze stared at Money. "I don't think it's soft," he said and shook his head in disbelief. "It's just everything that I saw today don't look that serious. It look like you making shit way more complicated than it is."

"Perception a mafucka ain't it?" Money said. "We'll holla at you. Be safe, and hit us up when you touch back on another visit."

Blaze got out and turned to the car.

Money looked at his childhood friend, at his brother, Blaze. "This a cold young world Blaze. You better adapt to this shit or you gon' die you this shit."

Blaze stood in the middle of the street and watched the car pull off.

Chapter 22

Money and Paper pulled up to the store Jared had sent them to, got out, walked the short distance and entered the clothing store. A Jamaican stepped from the back. He had a crown on his head, but it was easy to see that he had very long dreadlocks underneath. He approached the cash register and gave his attention to Money and Paper who were looking at the scarce clothing on the racks in the store.

"Are you finding everything okay?" The Jamaican asked.

Money moved a shirt on a rack and looked at a shirt. He looked at the clerk behind the counter. "Actually I'm here looking for A.D."

The man's eyes turned into slits behind the counter. He pull his cell phone to his lips and said a few words. Money and Paper approached the counter but froze when another man came from the back and stood next to the clerk.

"I'm A.D., who's looking for me?'

Money smiled with the colorful grill. "I'm Money, Jared sent me to do a favor." Money looked at the clerk. "2 favors actually."

The fat man eyed him suspiciously then said, "Come around the counter and follow me to the back so we can talk."

Money and Paper followed. In the back A.D. turned to them.

"Yeah, the 2 favors are a nigga named Banga and another nigga name CD. Cd ratting and Banga selling Jared's shit but skimming some of the profits off the top. Hold up real quick," AD told them and went to his desk, scribbled something on a pad and ripped the page off. He walked back over and gave it to Money. "You'll be able to find both of them at these addresses."

Money looked at the paper but didn't take. "No need," Money told him. "I know exactly where to find both of these niggas. I'll be in touch when everything is how it's supposed to be."

Money and Paper exited the clothing store.

Chapter 23

Money and Paper parked in the back of Banga's house. They knew he wouldn't be an easy job, after all he is the one that supplied their guns, and he supplied most of the neighborhood.

They both put on latex gloves and got out of the car.

They kept to the shadows as they moved towards the backdoor. Money twisted the knob but the door was locked. With a gloved hand Money knocked on the door and then stepped back and took his shooting stance with the gun up.

Footsteps came toward hem in the other side of the door and then they stopped. "Who is it?" A woman's voice asked on the other side of the door.

"C.D.," Paper said in a muffled voice then looked at Money and shrugged.

They heard the door unlock then watched the knob twist and the door open slowly. A woman stuck her face out. Money kicked the door as hard as he could. The woman flew backwards into the wall, hit her head, then fell to the floor and down the basement steps. They ran in with pistols up. When they reached a small hallway they stopped.

Money turned to Paper and whispered, "I'll open the doors on the left side and you do the other side. But go slow."

Paper nodded and veered over to his side of the dark hallway.

Money opened the first door on his side and gun first he entered the dark room. He was barely inside the room when he heard 3 gunshots. He ran out and to the other side of the hallway, to Paper's side, and through an open door. Paper was on the wall and holding his left shoulder. He followed Paper's eyes across the dark room. Banga was sprawled out on the floor in front of the closet. Money walked over and stood over Banga, took aim at the back of his head and pulled the trigger then went over and helped Paper up, out of the house, and out to the car then hurried back inside the house, this time he didn't go upstairs but down to the basement. He stopped where the woman was unconscious on the steps, aimed at her heart and pulled the trigger.

Chapter 24

Man Man and Cuz were on the south side parked at a mixtape store parking lot. They were smoking a blunt and watching the door of the mixtape store. They could see everyone that came and left. It didn't take long before they saw the man they had come to see.

The mixtape store's manager, CD.

CD walked out of the music shop, reached up for the gate, but froze when a pair of headlights shined on him. He turned just in time to see a pair of headlights, he heard a motor rev loudly. He raised his elbow and shielded his eyes from the bright headlights and the car smashed into him and made he was sandwiched between the brick wall. The car reversed. Burned rubber then skidded to a stop. CD's body fell to the ground and blood poured from his mouth. The BPN members burned rubber and sped off into the dark night.

They drove to an alley in an opposition neighborhood and dropped the car off, hopped in another car they had parked there and cruised down the alley with casually without drawing any attention to themselves.

They cruised all the way to the meet up spot they had set up with Money and Paper but when they got there and scoped out the scene it was clear as day that Money and Paper were nowhere to be found.

Chapter 25

Paper couldn't show up at the hospital with a gunshot wound because the cops would be called. Money took him to a nurse's house, she was from the hood but she fixed him up in less than an hour.

When Paper was all patched up they made their way to meet up spot where Cuz and Man Man were waiting for them.

#

At the meet up the BPN members smiled at the sight of their brothers. They were all glad that the mission had been accomplished and that everyone had made it back safely.

The news came on the tv. They all turned to the television and watched. The reporter was a slim white woman in a yellow coat tied by a blue belt at the waist.

:Bodies are popping up everywhere..." the news reporter reported. The clip was long but when the faces came up on the screen of the dead men that's when reality hit everyone in the room.

Money went to the bathroom, took a shower and got himself together.

Paper went next, then Man Man, and then Cuz. When they were all done they went outside to the backyard and to a 55 gallon metal drum and started a fire, then one by one all 4 BPN members walked up and tossed their clothes into the flames and watched as the only evidence to their crimes went up in flames.

#

The 2 detectives watched the gang members around the fire as they burned the clothes. There was a video camera on the dash recording the entire. The camera caught everything up into the point they went back into the meet up spot.

Chapter 26

When the time came all 4 BPN members exited the safe house and got in the car. They made their way to Jared's dealership. At the dealership only 2 of them got out, Money and Paper.

Inside jared was waiting for them in the lobby by his fancy cars and in a fancy suit. The men greeted one another and then Jared pulled out a piece of paper and gave it to Money.

"This is the address. The name you need is Mikey and the password is luxurious."

Money looked at the piece of paper then back up at Jared, he nodded then him and Paper turned and went back out to the car where Man Man and Cuz were waiting for them.

"Stop at the projects before we leave," Money told Paper who was behind the wheel.

Paper nodded then turned off and headed in the direction of the projects.

A block away from the project's south gate Paper slammed on the breaks and everyone in the car stared at the scene in front of them in shock. Police cars and raid vans were everywhere. BPN members were being hauled out of units and seated on the curb in handcuffs by the dozens.

"Get the fuck away from here," Money told Paper.

Paper reversed, did a U – turn then created distance between them and the scene in the projects. They were almost to the highway when a cop car got behind them and hit the red and blue lights on the roof.

Paper looked at Money. "What you want me to do?"

"Pull over. Might just a be a traffic stop, if not then it's his loss." Money told him looking in the rearview.

Paper pulled the car to the side of the road and they watched as the 2 cops got out and started for their car. At the back of the car the 2 cops split up, one went the driver side window and the other to the passenger side window. They both drew their guns and he cop on the driver's side knocked on the Paper's window.

Paper did what he was asked to do.

"License and registration please," The cop on the driver side asked Paper and waited. He bent and looked inside the car. First he scanned the front, then the backseat.

In the backseat his eyes froze on Man Man. Man Man lifted his gun and shot the cop in the face. His blood sprayed all over Paper behind the wheel. The other cop on side grabbed his pistol, but he wasn't fast enough. Money shot the cop under the chin.

Paper smashed on the gas and they fled the scene as fast as they could with the cop's blood smeared across the side of their car.

"We can't stay around here," Money said "I'm sure that everything blown up already anyway. Hit the highway."

Chapter 27

When they made it to Chicago they stopped at a gas station to get gas and Money went to the bathroom and called Tricia. She gave him the scoop on everything that had happened around town. She told him what he had already known, that the projects had been hit and that they'd raided all the safe houses. They raided the house where they lived as well as every other known or suspected BPN member.

Money knew that nothing would ever be the same again and that there was no going back to a normal life. Him and Tricia said their goodbyes and hung up.

#

In Chicago they found the address the leader of a Mexican gang BPN had affiliations with. The house was a little brownstone with a black van parked out front. That was their landmark. They parked behind the black van.

A man in a dark hoody got out and walked up to the car. He inside the passenger window and scanned the car. "You guys don't look like you're from around here." He said. His accent was Spanish and thick. "You need directions or something homes?"

Money gave the man the piece of paper from Jared. The man looked at it and said, "I'm about to get back in the van and I want you to follow me. We're going to the docks."

Before they got to the docks Money could see the boats and their sails sticking up high into the sky.

They followed the van until it stopped. The Spanish cat got out and motioned for Money and the rest of the BPN members to do the same.

They followed him to a garage door. He lifted the garage door and ushered the BPN members into the warehouse. In the center of the floor there was 8 Mexicans. They were standing around a U haul truck. All of them had on all black including black ski masks rolled up over their heads and black gloves, and all of them had big guns either on their waists or long assault rifles strapped across their bodies.

One of the Mexicans stepped forward and tossed Money the keys to the U haul. Money caught them. When he looked up the man's right hand was extended out to Money. Money took the hand and shook it.

Money turned and tossed he keys to Man Man the looked at Paper and said, "Bring the money over here."

Paper brought the money over gave it to the Mexican and the Mexican gave it to another man next to him that unzipped and scanned the cash inside then looked up and nodded.

"The title and insurance papers, everything is inside of the glove box. We don't need the truck back either. When you reach your destination just destroy that shit homes."

They shook hands again and Money and the BPN members climbed into their rental and the U-Haul and jumped on the highway.

Chapter 28

Money and Paper cruised the highway in the rental car 2 cars behind the U-Haul. They had followed it back from Chicago.

20 miles away from the Muskegon exit Money looked in the rearview mirror and saw 2 state trooper cars gaining speed on the highway behind them.

Money looked at Paper.

"It's a state trooper behind us a few cars back." When Money looked in the mirror again the trooper had advanced a couple of cars and was closer. He looked at Paper again. "They on us bro."

2 more dark blue state trooper SUV's joined the other troopers behind the BPN members. Money and Paper both gripped their pistols and waited for their moment to attack, but then the state troopers, like birds in flight, sped up and passed Money and Paper in their rental car and at 70 miles an hour converged on the U-Haul truck.

#

Paper pressed on the break a little as the police and the U-Haul sped up until it was a full fledged chase. Money and Paper watched in horror until the U haul tried to make the exit but was going to fast and flipped over. It flipped over on its roof and slid. Bright sparks flew everywhere. It came to a stop 50 yards down the exit ramp and the state troopers surrounded it quickly. They jumped out, 2 inside a truck and with their guns trained and aimed on the U haul.

Money and Paper kept took the Muskegon exit and as they went around the loop they watched unmarked black SUV's swarm the scene and men and women in FBI jumped out.

Chapter 29

Money and Paper parked the rental in the same spot they'd parked in the last time they had came to the clothing store to pay the owner a visit for Jared. They watched the entrances for a moment, and when the owner came out they were both there to meet him.

"Closing up kind of late ain't you?"

The owner jumped and spun toward the voice only to be staring down the barrel of both the guns in Paper and Money's hands. Money kicked the man in the stomach. He flew back, threw the door, and into the store then slid on the waxed floor.

"It was a set up my nigga," Money said and him and Paper stepped inside the store. They walked in and stood over him. 2 deathly shadows hovering over him and both with ill intent. "Feds at that."

Paper chimed in. "We get to the spot, meet with the right people and do all the right shit, but then out of nowhere on the way back, just 15 miles from the drop off, every state trooper on the road get on our ass. How the fuck is that possible?"

"Look young nigga," the store owner pleaded with his hands held outwards toward his assaulters. "I ain't got shit to do with no police. Feds, or local. I don't swing that way."

Paper grabbed the man by the ankle and drug him across the floor.

Money walked to the back of the shop where they had been the day before and Paper followed him with in his grip.

"Put that nigga in a chair," Money shouted.

Paper snatched the man up and tossed him in a chair, then grabbed some belts and strapped him to the chair with them while Money closed and locked the back door.

"Take whatever you want, just leave me alive, please," the man pleased.

Paper punched the man across the face with a stiff blow.

"7 – 5-" the man shouted out through bloody teeth.

Paper punched him again. Knocked more blood from his mouth.

"What the fuck you talking about?" Money shouted.

"The combination to the safe. It's 7 – 5 – 16. Please, just don't kill me. It's behind us on the wall, under the poster."

Paper punched the man again. Money went to the wall and snatched the picture off. He dialed the numbers the man had given them on the safe's keypad. The safe beeped, went silent, then popped open.

Money grabbed 2 kilos of heroin inside and returned to Paper and their hostage.

"What you get?" Paper asked.

"2 bricks of heroin," Money said and put his gun to AD's head and pulled the trigger.

chapter 30

5 Months Later

Everything associated with BPN had came crashing down. One day it was on top of the world and the next it was fighting for it's life.

There was no way Money or Paper could stay in Muskegon, there was simply too much heat, and their faces were too known and their crimes too heinous. They didn't stand a chance. They knew if the police by themselves didn't get them, they knew the reward money on their heads would surely help them get caught faster.

\#

Money and Paper got on a greyhound, they went to the state's capital, Lansing, and laid low. Money had stayed in Lansing once before and knew his way around, and he knew people if they needed to shoot any moves. Man Man and Cuz had went to some of their people's cribs down in Detroit but the shit with the Detroit niggas is what had set everything off and that didn't seem like a good idea to Money neither. There was nothing better than Lansing.

It had been 5 months but word had come through the BPN information pipeline that Jared, the bad realtor, had resurfaced, and that was bad for Jared because he was on the BPN hit list and had a green light on his head. Money knew it had to be done right and knew he couldn't send anyone else by word through the information pipeline because that would waste too much time and Jared might slip away again. Plus the job had to be done right and had to be done fast and that meant Money and Paper had to go themselves.

#

They met Man Man in an abandoned house deep on the south side of Muskegon and right off the highway. It was risky but they snuck into the city. The car dealership was less than 2 minutes away from the bando, and the highway was less than a minute away from both locations.

Money and Paper were already inside when Man Man materialized in the shadows of the abandoned house's kitchen. "It's me," he said and lowered his gun.

There was someone behind him.

"Come in," Money said and ushered him inside. "That's Cuz with you?"

The person with Man Man removed the hood from his head and stuffed the Gun down the front of his pants.

Man Man pointed to the stranger. "Cuz couldn't' make it but this my cousin from the city. Good nigga, and he get down just like us. Ruthless."

Money and Paper studied the stranger with their gunshot their hands. Studied his black clothes, his cold stare, and then at the front of his pants where he'd put the pistol.

"What's your name bro?" Money asked and turned the stranger's way. He was in the man's face. They could feel one another's breath on their skin.

"Skee," he said and extended his hand out to Money. "And you must be Money."

Money hesitantly shook Skee's hand. "Yeah, that's me," Money said, "But they call me Young World." He smiled and flashed his colorful teeth. They glistened in the faint light inside the abandoned house. "You BPN?" Money asked him.

Skee shook his head. "Nope, DTM, out of Detroit. We got a coalition with BPN though."

Paper stepped to Skee but spoke to Man Man. "You vouching for this nigga Man Man?"

Man Man looked at Skee the back at Money then back to Paper and sucked his teeth. "We grew up together. Was real close before I moved to down Muskegon. It was only natural that we came right back together when I touched back down. We peoples and gone always be peoples. Plus he with the shi-"

"Nigga is you vouching for him!" Paper repeated.

"Yeah nigga, I'm vouching for him. I don't know what type of shit Cuz on, but he basically backed out. I ain't seen the nigga in a week. Just disappeared."

Money flipped the hood back over his head. "Let's go."

The others flipped the hoods over their heads and followed Money out the back door and to the van parked down the alley a ways down.

Chapter 31

It didn't take long to get to Jared's car dealership and once there they parked and got out with their guns drawn. They slipped masks over their faces and started for the door.

Money snatched door open, ran inside and swept the wide expanse of the dealership where the cars were with his gun, the others were right behind him.

Money stopped and looked at the office door. There was light coming from underneath it and low soft music coming from behind it. He motioned with his head to the door and all 4 men surrounded it. Money turned the knob and pulled it open.

Jared had a woman bent over his desk, his pants were around his ankles, and he was fucking her brains out next to a pile of cocaine and a fifth of Jack Daniels.

Money shot the woman in the face. She fell to the desk with Jared's dick still inside her. Jared screamed hysterically with blood on his face and hands.

"What the fuck!" Jared finally managed. He was high as a kite.

Paper put his pistol to Jared's head and without a word he pulled the trigger then he turned to Money with the smoking gun and a smile on his face. The smile quickly faded.

Skee had his gun on both Man Man and Money. He shot them both then turned to Paper.

Paper pulled the trigger.

Nothing happened.

Skee laughed and pulled the trigger. The explosion was loud and the bullet hit Paper in the neck. He fell backwards, over the desk then crashed to the floor. On the ground he grabbed at his neck and gurgled on his own blood. Skee walked over to Man Man, put his foot on his back and stopped Paper from crawling for his gun just a few feet away. He unloaded his clip in Paper's back and legs.

Whistling and Skee walked around and looked down at Money. "Big World was my cousin nigga." Skee said while changing his clip. When it was he chambered a bullet then pulled back on the trigger 5 times. No shots sounded off though just the click of the empty chamber.

Money coughed up blood.

"Fuck!" Skee snapped and looked around the floor and at the bodies frantically for another gun but the sirens were getting louder and louder which meant the cops were getting closer and closer. He kicked Money in the ribs again. Money cried out in agonizing pain. "Hopefully your bitch ass bleed out. Lucky mothafucka." He said then turned and ran out the door they had came in, took the van and bounced in the opposite direction of the sirens.

Chapter 32

Money's eyes jerked open and he looked around. It was obvious he was in a hospital. His eyes fluttered a few times then stayed open permanently. He knew he was lying down. He turned his head and looked through the open door and out into the hallway. Nurses and doctors walked by I both directions.

Then everything that had happened started coming back to him. He sat up frantically in the hospital bed and swung his feet over the edge of the bed. He was glad they worked. He remembered the bullets that had entered his body and looked down.

He opened the hospital gown and stared at the long jagged scar down zig zagging down the middle his stomach and closed up by staples. He went to reach for the jagged scar with his right hand but couldn't. Slowly he looked to the right and tears instantly welled up in his eyes. He was handcuffed to the hospital bed.

A nurse entered the room. When she saw him up and alert she didn't say a word, just turned and exited just as fast. She came right back, but this time there were 2 men with her, and they had on shirts with big yellow letters on the front that read FBI.

Money looked past the agents to the door at the 2 local detectives that had bagged Blaze. Money closed his eyes and shook his head. He knew his life was over.

Chapter 33

6 Months Later

Federal courtrooms are known for being huge in size compared to the crowds that they hold inside them. No one shows up to federal sentencing dates. Tricia and Alicia were in the front row. There was no one else inside the courtroom except for the US Marshals in the pews.

The judge looked up from the files in front of him then down at Money, then to the lawyer. "Is there anything you would like to say before I hand down sentencing?" The judge asked.

Money's lawyer got to his feet, looked at Money then up at the judge. "Your honor I would just like to say that my client is a good kid that went down a few wrong streets in life. Things have happened, and may have spiraled out of control but-"

The judge held up a hand and puckered his lips.

"With all due respect councilman, but this is not a kid." He pointed at Money, "This is far from a kid. This is a menace to society. I will not allow you to use youth as an excuse to run around and commit atrocious crimes against humanity and against the people of this community."

The judge looked out in the audience and addressed the US Marshals present. "Does the US Marshal service have the other defendant here today as well?"

One of the US Marshalls got to his feet and clasped his hands in front of his cheap black suit and nodded. "Yes judge."

Just then the courtroom's back door opened and 2 marshals pushed Paper into the courtroom. He was in a wheelchair and the wheelchair. The Marshal pushed Paper to the front and parked him next to Money and his lawyer.

The judge continued. "Now that both defendants are present we'll commence with the sentencing…"

Neither Money or Paper heard a single word that came out of the judge's mouth. Non of the small talk. Nothing but the years that came out but those years weren't actually years but letters.

"L -I -F -E," the judge said casually. He smacked his gavel on the bench and stared down and out at the 2 young men he had just condemned to the rest of their days in the penitentiary. Maybe the judge was the smartest man in the entire situation, because despite his position and what side of the law he's on he is the only one that truly understands best the weight and severity of the world.

The US Marshals escorted Money and Paper out of the courtroom. There were no words and goodbyes allowed and no hugs and kisses. No warmth at all. Just 2 teenagers hauled off to rot in a living and breathing factory.

#

In federal prison it usually takes a few weeks to ride out, and sometimes maybe a few months.

Money and Paper were held together the entire time and were thankful for it because they knew that once they got to where they were going, which was ADX they wouldn't ever see each other again, let alone another soul for many years to come.

They stood on the side of the bus on the runway and waited to board the airplane that the feds used to transport people, or Con-air.

When the. Arsenal called Money and Paper's names they both climbed the stairs of the airplane with the shackles biting at their ankles, but when they were on the airplane there was a big mean looking US Marshal with a mean mug on his face and a list in his hand screaming out orders and grabbing inmates and pushing them into empty seats of his choice. He grabbed Money's tiny frame and pushed him toward the back.

"You back there and sit to the right." Then he grabbed Paper. Paper fought but was still weak from his wounds and shackled. The US marshal pushed him back toward the front of the airplane. "You go back that way and to the left."

Money and Paper looked at one another in the aisle of the airplane. Just stared until they were pushed apart by a US Marshal. They didn't have a clue she. They would see each other again.

#

At his window seat in the airplane Money watched the runway as the plane took off and lifted in the sky.

For Money life had been short, cold, and had taken him places that he there is no return from.

As the airplane punched through the clouds Money knew that he had to come up with a plan to change his life just like he had done on the street. Either that or he would just be a victim of a cold young world.

EPILOGUE

Present Day

Money looked at the youngster with tears welled up in his eyes but he refused to let them fall. He dared not to. He had an image to uphold and one of his organization members were in his face so he dared not let him see him cry. If he was going to cry it would be later and behind closed doors where no one could see him.

Money looked out of the window as the plane descended through the clouds and started began its landing. He wasn't free by a long shot but wherever he was going was better than ADX.

He turned back to the young member. "That's the story. The whole truth. Nothing added and nothing taken out. Cold hard facts."

The youngster looked at Money with so much respect it couldn't be described by words if Money tried to explain the look to someone else.

A wide smile crawled over the youngster's face. "Damn OG, you been through it. You niggas represented for the Mob though."

Money held up his shackled hands and shook his head simultaneously. "If you call this representing for the Mob then your thinking fucked up, and if the whole Mob think like that, then the whole mob fucked up. My nigga, this ain't living or representing." Money let the words linger in the airplane seat between him and the youngster. "This ain't gangsta, gangsta is the next level."

The US marshalls boarded the plane with lists in their hands of people that were getting off of the plane and on to their next destination.

While everyone else focused up front Money leaned close to the youngster so that he could hear him. "Listen lil homie, the goal is to be present in every situation of life that our loved ones, brothers, and people might need us in. Behind these walls, in these chains and shackles, my nigga we ain't no help."

The marshal at the front of the plane called Money's name out. In handcuffs, belly chains, and leg irons, Money got to his feet and stepped out into the aisle of the airplane, but he didn't take a step. He turned to the youngster and through up BPN.

"Represent the right way," he smiled. "I'll see you on the other side, and when I do, we'll make more history. Only this time we do it together."

The youngster threw up BPN and nodded. "On the other side Big Homie."

Money turned and was escorted down the aisle and off the airplane with his chains rattling and his head held up high.

The End...

About The Author

Robert D. Williams is the most versatile and creative writer in America today. He is the author of the Must Keep a Gun series, The duffel bag short story collection, and the Thug Motivation series. Robert is a movie buff, has OCD when it comes to his writing, is an avid reader, and is a Michigan native.

To contact him hit him up at: oneshotpublications@gmail.com.

Made in the USA
Monee, IL
28 July 2021